LOST VOICES OF HORROR

J T Shields

House 13 Publications

Copyright © 2022 J T Shields

All rights reserved

The characters and events portrayed in this book are fictitious. Any similarity to real persons, living or dead, is coincidental and not intended by the author.

No part of this book may be reproduced, or stored in a retrieval system, or transmitted in any form or by any means, electronic, mechanical, photocopying, recording, or otherwise, without express written permission of the publisher.

ISBN-13: 9798798869602
ISBN-10: 1477123456

Cover design by: Art Painter
Library of Congress Control Number: 2018675309
Printed in the United States of America

To Jess.

Thank you for everything.

CONTENTS

Title Page
Copyright
Dedication
Things not done   1
Augmented   8
In the blood   16
The House with three walls   31
Boardwalk   44
Tommy   63
The phone call   75
Memory of a hen party   85
Grand breakfast   99
Clones   120
The Kronos   128
The Old Man   136
Black Fox   160

THINGS NOT DONE

Late afternoon in the city, the kind in which heat hangs around the concrete, distorting the air ahead as the street gasps for breath. I'd walked this way a hundred times or more. The same shop fronts, the bustling bus stops and hum of traffic, which should have been a perfect fit of familiarity for the contours of my brain. It wasn't. It was all so different. Tiredness warped my senses, creating an uncomfortable world of sharp edges. The things I knew had become additional barriers to traverse. The world hadn't changed. I had.

It was my first journey out with the baby. The bouncing buggy shook my arms, wheels caught against the curb-stones, throwing my body forward painfully into the contraption. At that moment I heard the baby stir, it's lungs preparing for battle once again. I moved more quickly, despite the dizziness, the throbbing against my eyes and the ripeness of my sweat pulling clothes closer. Aware of the springs, the shiny metal legs and multitude of unfathomable clips hanging from this new wheeled appendage, all I could do was trundle forward.

Of course, we attended all the classes, read all the books. Birth plans carefully drawn up, all the things we could possibly need, I ticked off checklists and readied around the house.

The birth had been three days of pain and anxiety. Coffee had seen him through the hospital, the uncertainty and the inability to do anything. He was useless. When he took my hand, his fingers slipped with drowsiness, his eyes partly shutting. Still, I squeezed at his skin, hating him through gritted teeth and clenched bones.

The midwife said we could go. We wandered back to the car less than a day after its emergence. On that careful drive home, my hands resting against a tiny body, it all seemed manageable. Then came the screaming. That's when I knew. An empty heart lurked in the shadows of my smile. An unpleasantness, I'd wanted to confess from the moment they had thrust its body against my skin. Surely, we should have a connection, some positive reinforcement of my choice to have a child? Instead, the wailing from quivering jaws created a thickening in my throat. I whispered. Still, it screamed.

In the absence of sleep, I walked. At first pacing the house, this tiny creature in my arms. Its cries bouncing off the walls. Always returning, pushing into the tissue of my brain. The pressure building until I knew it would burst. In the hallway, still unused, I looked at the pram.

"I'm going out with it," I call. He looks at me. There was no light in his eyes, only rings of darkness.

The steady rock, the gentle squeak of springs, the rumble

of tyres, lulled the cry into whimpering and eventually nothing. Still, I pushed, my pulse racing against the stillness. At the edges of my sight, everything fluttered out of focus, leaving me with a single tunnel of clarity. I had to keep moving.

I ploughed through high street shoppers. My reflection was a skimming stone against the shop windows until I found myself outside of Morgan's Music. Guitars hung at jaunty angles behind the display. A piano sat at the forefront, its shiny black casement fresh and polished as my own had once been. I often stopped to enjoy the instruments. Finally, a moment of familiarity. It was ridiculous to admit; I saw a life I had never chosen behind that glass. I often wondered what if? Usually, I'd bask in the faraway melancholy for a moment, reflecting on that single decision. A moment in which I'd let that possibility slip away. Only now, it was overwhelming. A sadness so intense it cut into me, scraping against my ribs and compressing my lungs. In my shudder, the light caught against the window, the instruments disappeared and I'm left with an even more sorrowful vision.

I saw myself. Suddenly, that's all I could focus on: the translucent figure, hair wild, body bloated in the storefront's reflection. Too unlike my mirror image to accept. I reached my hand across the window, wanting to sweep away the illusion. The distorted double reached out to me. Our fingertips touched. If I could have fallen away for a moment, I imagined I would have. To float in the warped viscosity observing the world. Only the muffled hum of life getting through. The other me looked back. Oh, the frenzied drumming of my heart at that drowning. The space inside my head closed in, wrapping my thoughts into the sudden horror of myself.

Baby cried. Surely, I had only been a moment. Its shrillness drifted into my display, tugging at me. Heads turned in my direction. Angry faces whispered to one another. People stopped walking to see my neglect.

"I'm not fucking killing it!" I wanted to shout, but I didn't.

Instead, I continued on jellied legs and sinking feet, while the laser eyes burned across my back.

"Don't cry," My motherless words were empty on the air. Everybody would know we were imposters forced together.

Darkness saved me from it all. A narrow alleyway led away from the pounding feet of shoppers. The smell of piss stung my nose as soon as I'd pushed the pram into the confines. Urine splash marks decorated the brickwork, still seeping into a foamy stream.

I carried on. The passage twisted around on itself, sloping, darkening like the spiral of a helter-skelter taking me deeper. We passed under a tunnel. Cries echoed against the dark and my gritted teeth. I emerged, my eyes blinded at the sudden glare. I pulled the pram to a halt.

Canals don't make the rushing sound of a river as it meanders against nature's banks. Instead, there is a stillness as the water sits thick, unmoving, murky against the afternoon sun. The city's filth leached through drainage pipes, releasing a powerful odour of decay across the walkways. The wheels of the pram sat on the edge of the bank. Another step, or a less secure grip, could have seen the fabric and metal sink under the water. The front wheels span freely as they rested off the ground.

Looking around, at first I think I'm alone, except for the screeching creature balancing on the edge of the canal. This baby ripped into the hidden, peeling and scraping at who I was. It was the first time it had been the two of us. I moved the pram away from the water and reached inside for the baby. Her body fragile against my own. Not for the first time, so many worries push down against me.
Somebody watched. She stood on the opposite side, looking into the rippling water as it bubbled in front of her. The

baby moaned, the gentle bouncing in my arms a useless gesture, showing me up against the stranger. Jostling, my fingers slipping, I try to speak to the thing in my arms with inaudible murmurs. As I move the bundle from one arm to the next, trying to support every part of its body, its cries grew louder.

The woman glared, a statue not even responding to my weak smile, quickly thrown at her. The odd bubble still popped on the surface in front of where she stands, while the rest of the canal is deathly still. My walk, with both hands held against the child, became a display as her watchful scowl crawled across my skin.

"There, there," I say. The words are odd and pointless on my tongue. My mouth opens too soon so I can't think of what to say next.

Instead, I glance back at the woman. My stomach turning over, my tired brain already processing the details I'd not wanted to admit. She stood in the same position, only her head moving with me. I couldn't make out her face across the bank, the distance distorting the features, but I noticed the way her clothes billowed around her, caught in a non-existent breeze.

"Hello," I called across the water. The baby's voice shrill against my own. Shadows danced across my peripheral vision, my feet stuck against an imaginary sponge floor. The woman doesn't respond. Against my drumming heart, I call out to her again. "Are you okay?"

The woman stepped forward, feet on the concrete lip of the canal, her hands clutching at the air in front of her. Her hair, floating out around her head, her mouth moving, the dark exterior on show before snapping shut, like a fish gasping for air.

"Do you need help?" I call. My scalp prickled. I pulled the child closer into my body as I moved back towards the pram.

It's when I lay my child down, I notice she is no longer

crying. Instead, there is a tiny smile across her rapid breaths. I ran my fingers across her cheek. The tears press at the corners.

When I turn, ready to leave, the woman no longer stands across from me. Instead, the space is menacing, the unreality, the emptiness too real, crackling in my ears like a distorted frequency. It's easy to imagine the last trace of the woman still occupying the moment. Each of my steps, rolling forward with the cushioned rubber of the pram's wheels, until I reach the edge of the bank myself and peer into the unfathomable murk, afraid of what I'll see.

There is only the shimmering of the Sun's dying light. Dazzling lines of white across the film of water. I noticed more. The reflection of an overhanging plant is visible, squeezing its way to life through the tightly packed mortar of the pathway. I leaned closer. A throbbing beat inside my head growing louder. My legs, weak beneath my body.

At first it was an outline, rising from below. Only a few centimeters of the water was clear enough to make out any detail. That's where the body lay. A tangled heap of hair flowed across her face. The tendrils, a shade darker than my own, swept forward across her open mouth and obscured her eyes, working against the flow of the water. Her arm, hands, fingers reached out, grasping towards me as she floated.

I fell back, not able to see anymore. My shoes scraped against the ground, propelling me backwards to give me as much distance from the bank as possible. I clutched at air before taking hold of the buggy's handle, unable to unlock my stare. At any moment, I expected to see the woman levitate into view. It's thin arms dragging a connected torso out of the water. There I stood. Gasping, my lungs struggled to get air, fighting as I spluttered uncontrollably. Finally, I backed away with my hands controlling the handle.

My eyes never left the canal as I started back through the underpass. That was the worst part. The stillness of it all suffocated me. As though it had always been like this and nothing had happened at the waterside. Any movement, any sound was with me. After I left, I could imagine the emptiness of it all, existing for nobody to see. Before I stood on the edge, there were only vacated towpaths and the secrets of the water's muddy depths.

I called the police the moment I got home. I couldn't have done it any sooner. Emma needed feeding. After this, she fell back to sleep. A small patch of vomit splashed against my shoulder. I sat, listening to Simon snore, and Emma's breath against the folds of my arm. They create a rhythm washing over me like lapping water. My muscles unpicking through dizzying weariness, I collapsed deeper into the sofa. I didn't have the energy to lay her down. Instead, I remain seated in our living room, submerged in darkness. Haunted by the things I hadn't done, I let the numbing calmness drown me.

I wondered if the police would ever find a body.

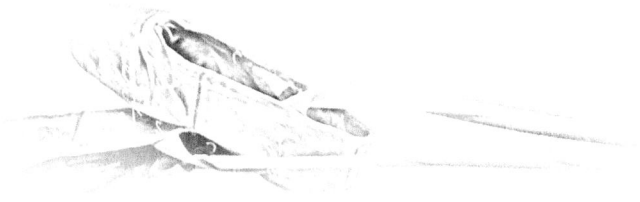

AUGMENTED

Mark scattered the paperwork across the dining table. He had kept everything in a bulging manila envelope. An order of service with Annie's young face slid onto the surface. It was one of the first proof copies he had checked over. It was quickly buried under the mound of forms, bills and even the glossy catalogue of caskets which tumbled out after it. Finally, he found what he was looking for, tucked into the final correspondence from the funeral directors. A narrow black leaflet he'd thought little about at the time. Just another of the commodities of death along with the brochures on keepsake necklaces and remembrance books.

"Want to see your memories come back to life? Our aug-

mented reality process can help you say goodbye at a speed that's right for you." Sweaty hands distorted the ink around the edges of the glossy paper.

Laura was still in bed regardless of the day's lateness. Despite efforts, his words couldn't break through the thick, stale air as she groaned against the duvet. They, like him, were intruders in a tomb. She looked at him through watery eyes as he sat on the bed. Dry lips opened slightly.

How much of this was down to him?

There was nothing he wanted more than to climb in next to her, close his eyes and block out the world forever. An impossibility he couldn't achieve.

"Why don't you just talk to me?" She had become a broken radio, only able to communicate with static. "Tell me how you feel. Discuss what we do next. Anything. Please."

"Not now. Mark. I can't…" She covered her forehead with her hands.

"When then? It's been two years. We've barely existed with each other since it happened. Everything about you has changed. The way you act, the things you do, even how you move. We can't go on like this Laura."

"You mean you can't go on like this Mark." Words spat out. Hands contained her thoughts, entombing all that she was.

"It's not healthy for anybody." Mark's voice was a fire spreading; his words tumbled like burning embers. "It's not just you Laura. I've lost our baby too, but you're not helping. You're making everything worse. You're destroying us. Don't you understand!" Mark was on his feet; he was standing over Laura, his face fraught, spittle bursting from his mouth. When he paused, he realised she was sobbing. That pain of loss, the withdrawal from each other, brought him down.

"I'm so sorry." Bent over, his face close, more intimate than he had been for a long time, he wanted to touch her, to run his fingers across her cheek but was uncertain about the contact.
"It was so sudden. She was just gone. I never got to see her fade or have some kind of goodbye." Her voice torn. "Mark, why is it I can't dream of her? I can't see her running around, or smiling or being at home. I just want to see her again. Why can't I see her again?"

Those words reverberated through him. They mocked him until there was little choice. Mark held the paper for a long time. The slogan *"Want to see your memories come back to life?"* rested above an image of an elderly couple dancing, a head cradled on a shoulder. Younger members of the family watched on with smiles painted across their faces. It was an image that sickened him.

Eventually, he made the call.

Laura was hiding in the darkness of their bedroom again. Mark was alone; he thumbed the container while the sofa enveloped him. Six years of life transferred through videos and live photos; the box had arrived after only two weeks. The rehearsed words had disappeared before he had recited them to Laura. They had become his secret. Unclipping the cardboard tube, he revealed a small grey case. Inside were two glasses. The smooth white frames, and simplicity of it all appealed. He put them on.

There was a slight green tinge through the glass, objects, the floors, the ceiling all coated in the light before fading. Then it was back to how it always had been. The patio window caught the afternoon sun as it spilt across the carpet. Annie was not there. He released the breath he hadn't been aware of holding. Fingertips rested on the frames.

Then there she was.

Annie was in the light, looking at Mark. Even though she had never attended a ballet class, she wore that tatty ballerina dress with threadbare stockings and frayed hem. There was movement too. The replication of his daughter mimicked even the basics of life with the verisimilitude of respiration. Each inhalation caused her little chest to move. Her face frozen in time. Stood in front of the sun, not casting a shadow was the six-year-old he had lost.

Mark wrenched backwards, his body coiled tightly against itself. Annie tilted her expressionless face towards him. Eyes followed his momentum while lashes blinked. The same eyes that had left the world two years ago. He climbed on the couch, his feet sinking into the fabric like loose soil absorbing pressure. His brain reacted by pulling at the glasses, sending them tumbling into the cushioned comfort of the flooring. Annie was gone. Separation flooded against him.

Of course, Annie hadn't been there. The software reassembled the data and remade the image to evoke something elaborate and alive. A memory of theirs caught in a performance. Never would he use it again; he felt the shame, but yet his promise couldn't stop him. The lenses compelled him to return.

The living portrayal of Annie could walk around, dance and even respond to the wearer of the glasses. It was her! The same smile, and long blond hair hanging to one side over her shoulder. Annie stopped and waved at him before running out of the room; he could almost hear the ghostly feet pad across the flooring.   Silvery laughter, a ribbon looping around the house was practically audible. When she walked over to him, he could see every detail as he leaned in close; the slight cracking of skin on her lip, a minute scar above her eye, the eyelashes fluttering and those deep brown eyes, so rich and full as they looked back into his own. Portraits in the past gave impressions of life through eyes that followed or the artists' mastery, but none could match this reconstruction.

The longer he spent with her, the more he understood. When he was alone, he could find reassurance in the augmented reality created by technology. She mouthed the words he longed to hear, the corners of her lips twisted just as Annie had always done. There were times when they just sat with the other, him reading the news, Annie content with her presence in a way he hadn't seen before.

One night, while Laura had been restlessly asleep, Mark had heard her. The little footsteps in the corridor, like he had savoured when there was a child in their lives. Slipping out of bed, he followed the sound. It was easy to convince himself of his consideration by keeping the lights off, but the reality was he wanted to hide. Everything was still, so the very walls vibrated with the absence of noise. There was something else, a familiarity which was not a normal part of his home. The closer he got to the stairs, the more he recognised it. An odour muted by refrigeration and muffled by chemicals. It was the scent of slowed decomposition he had experienced with each trip to his daughter.

Her body waited for him, expectantly in a room without windows. A frugal bunch of flowers had floated in a glass vase, the white petals as pure as Annie's dress. The prolonged wait for the funeral date had caused her body to decompose with every visit until he could no longer see her. A rotten recollection, he couldn't remove.

"Daddy?" The tinkling chime of her voice called to him from the darkness waiting at the bottom of the stairs.

The muscles of his legs burned as he continued endlessly down. Then there she was, emerging from the nothingness. Face uncharacteristically stern, with eyes that fixed onto his own, locking him in place. Eyes that weren't as they had been, but had become aged, full of a regret beyond her years as they absorbed him.

A coldness ran through his body. Her hair hung differently to how he remembered, almost reversed like a mirror image of the girl he knew. Tentative footsteps felt spongy as he slid onto the hard floor, her face looming closer as she took a step forward. Everything slowed, so that his time was an eternal impression of her closing in on him, a never-ending state of sadness. The apparition mouthed something at him, the movement beyond anything he could comprehend, but he could see the urgency and pain. The skin around her jaws stretched into a silent, phantom scream.

Annie raised her arms towards him in expectation. They spread out wide with fingers apart like she wanted lifting. The need inside to hold her and cradle his child once again expanded. To hear her name, or see her smile simply because he was there, purely because she loved him unconditionally and she knew he would always keep her safe. He would stop the bad things from happening.

Only he hadn't.

It wasn't her anymore; he could see that now. It was an unconvincing imitation of life parading in front of him. It was too stiff, too unnatural.

Mark couldn't breathe.

Hands slipped through time as things moved once again. His lungs fought for air as he extended his hands towards the glasses.

They weren't there.

Annie launched herself. It was impossible to understand. Movement distorted. She was above. She consumed him. There was little he could do. Cowering down on the stairs, a stifled scream struggled forth. He gasped for air. Outstretched arms grabbed. In amongst the struggle, his voice emerged. An animalistic howl, from deep inside, surrendered part of him. It pushed itself free, up out of his strained throat in a horrific bulge of panic.

Annie was gone.

He collapsed backwards, his body a pinched muscle of pain and perturbation that wheezed in the isolating darkness of the bottom of the stairs. Mark cried tears he hadn't realised he'd saved. Unable to think beyond the swell of fear which gripped the pounding electrical impulses of his brain. Even though she was gone, her presence still lingered.

It was then he felt the cold hands around him. They moved across his neck, edging over his shoulders until they met across his chest. The hands closed and knitted firmly. The touch, the texture of her skin, the weight of those hands on his body pushed against him. A new fear, outside of his experience, held on to his gasping lungs. Impulse pulled him away as he grabbed the flesh of her hands with his own.

"Annie?" He turned to face this creature, stepping backwards, only his daughter wasn't there.

"I know," Laura said. "Let it out." She moved towards him. "I heard. You're in pain. I've known we have both been suffering and now we can begin to heal. I've been waiting for you to feel the loss, Mark." Her hands squeezed him in a way they hadn't done for a long time bringing their grief together.

They walked up, back to their bedroom. Laura had a new optimism; she saw a world ahead just beginning to reopen because they could at last face recovery. It was the conception of their future.

Little did they know, it was the birth of pure evil.

IN THE BLOOD

Not all funeral processions gathered a crowd in our village, but this one did. Of course, I went out to stand amongst the others, even though Mama had told me not to. The black cart clattered down the centre of the road, pulled by two ebony horses, their muscles taut and powerful, lungfuls of air falling around them in clouds of white. Rev. Micheal's coffin, shrouded with purple, visible through the glass. Old Maid Addington's carriage followed behind. Dressed in black, her yellow skin and white hair falling about her. She turned, catching sight of me as it trundled on. Large, spindly wheels whirled, their spokes a blur. I imagined myself falling in, my arms spinning and snapping as it ate me up. Then it was gone. The coffin, flowers, the driver had all passed without an opportunity to take them in fully, so I started moving with the line of villagers towards the church. Our bodies huddled together. For once, I felt part of something more.

"Here," a whisper, a delicate touch on my palm, a tiny fold of parchment pressed inside. Jacob walked next to me. He didn't turn, but focused on moving with the procession. My glance was fleeting, catching his strong features and the manly whiskers forming on his chin. If his heart raced as fast as mine, he gave little sign.

"Amy, get yourself here girl, right this minute mind." Mama was at the doorway to our cottage, hands-on-hips and a frown painted on her face. Martha Knox, the innkeeper's wife, looked in her direction, surprised by her raised voice. She pulled her two small children closer, wrapping them in the folds of her cloak, making the sign of a cross with the tips of her fingers on her chest. Mama had scrapped her hair up into a bunch and tied it off with a red ribbon, but all this did was highlight the disarray. Greys fell in streaks like lines of ash across the otherwise dark mass. Tightly bunched sleeves held themselves high on her arms, while patches of flour stood out against her apron.

I don't remember what I said, but whatever it was it just made her more furious as I stomped away from the mourners and back to our cottage. She shook her fists at me until I relented, approaching the threshold with more than a little fear. I even ducked my head in expectation as I passed through the doorway, but she didn't lash out, not this time. Instead, she bore into me with her blue eyes until they congested my head with dizziness, thick against my aching brain. Ever since then, every headache I've ever experienced recognises that moment, her foot tapping on the quarry tiles, the smell of pastry slightly overbaked, my cheeks flushed against the heat of our home and embarrassment. I'm sure it didn't last all that long, but at that age, every moment is an eternity. Especially with the tiny scrap from Jacob folded into my fist, beating its own rhythm.

Did she know? Had she seen our delicate caress?

We spent our afternoons reading together in the small front room. During the winter, the logs cracked in the fire, drawing my attention more than anything inside the dusty volumes Mama kept on the shelves. My eyes growing heavy until her gravelly voice corrected me.

"Reading is a luxury, girl. Not to be wasted." Her voice shook me back into the room. I tucked myself up in the armchair and glared at her over the top of my book. The frustration, the burning injustice of not being able to see the funeral with everybody else, I expressed in my reading, turning the thin pages over with as much vehemence as possible, disappointed that Mama was oblivious to my protests.

At this time, I often felt drawn to stories of knights and dragons fighting for the heart of a princess, not that there were many of that type to choose from. Turning back to the story, I attempted to read a little more, but Jacob occupied my thoughts. Two pages on and I hadn't taken in any of the story. Mama squinted at her open book, an outstretched finger dragging along the cream pages, pausing and then continuing its journey with the same slowness.

Eventually, Mama heaved herself up from her chair, shaking her head and grumbling under her breath. No doubt at my reading choice. She placed her own reading material back on a shelf, cast an eye over my shoulder, and made her way to the door.

No sooner had she left, did I unwrap the delicate folds of Jacob's note. The faded desire to confront her reshaped with the sight of his markings. To have her treat me as a little girl when clearly a young lady sat in front of her, no longer seemed the right of it. Jacob's promise clear, not that he could write more than his name, but the symbol of his heart and the crescent moon told me what I needed to know. We would meet that very night and seal our bond with each other. Once done, they could not set it aside. I rehearsed some dialogue, my stomach filled with delicately flapping wings. She may not agree, but a final acknowledgement of my womanhood would be permission enough. There I sat, while the kettle whistled and Mama busied herself in the kitchen.

Finally, she wheeled the trolly in with the promised afternoon tea. I pushed Jacob's declaration in amongst the pages of the book and my bookmark, and snapped the volume shut as she approached. One look at the collection of small cakes and freshly baked bread subdued my discontentment. Mama always allowed more of a conversation after we had sampled her baking. She was tentative, pushing a teaspoon around a saucer, piling sandwiches onto my plate without regard, lost in other thoughts. It was then she told me her secret.

"Amy," she began, her attention now drifting to the window and the cold winter sunshine. I could feel the importance of what she intended to say in the air, like the invisible weight of the sun's rays pressing down on us. Ignoring this, I continued to fill myself with pastries, intending to hold back until she had her own say.

"It is time to talk. I know that." She sighed.

"Mama," I began. My resolve to wait shrivelled like burning bark. The remnants of sticky jam falling over my chin as I struggled in the direction I wanted to travel. "I am of woman age." My voice more childlike than ever. "There are things to discuss."

"I see, child." She sounded dismissive. I bit my lip at this, ready to interrupt, but she waved a hand at me.

"Not all of us are born the same as the next." She began moving the spoon around, pulling out the liquid from the bottom of the cup, only to let it drain onto the surface of the tea. "There are those rules for the top and different rules for bottom, girl. Some have power, while others collapse under it."

I nodded. A habit of mine at such an age was to agree with things, whether or not I understood them, especially if it didn't seem that interesting.

"Mama, does this have anything to do with the Old Maid Addington?" I asked. The words constructed by my unengaged brain, sticking at the borders of my cheeks as they passed into the room. No sooner than they had left my mouth, did I regret my way of asking. Once again, Mama fixed me with her steely stare, the purple veins around her nose and cheeks showing up more prominently because of the flushed colour they had become.

"Don't you go shaming me, girl. We don't refer to folks in such a way. Lady Addington is the way of it, I'll hear you say."

"Sorry, Mama." She bridled in her chair and then bent down to the bottom of the trolly where she produced the small silver cup and jug. Always a sign she was preparing me. Mama poured a cloudy liquid into the cup. Once full, she passed it over carefully.

"Drink, girl. It will do you some good."

I raised it hesitantly.

"Mama, does it have to be today?" I couldn't stand Jacob waiting and me not being able to join him.

"Hush up. You'll never blossom with questions." The frown on her face loosened as I pressed it against my mouth. The cup fuller than than she had ever offered before. The sticky substance clung thickly against my lips. They tingled pleasantly as I rubbed them together, dry despite the moisture.

"Yes, drink. All is well." She said. Her foot rocking impatiently as I drained the last. She peeled it from my hands and looked into the bottom of the cup, clicking her tongue as she peered inside. Her lips pursing as she shifted to look at me. A radiance filled my belly, smoothing the coursness of her voice as she continued.

"Way back now, girl, before you entered the world, I came across a mess of a child. Left alone, all scrawn and mud. Shunned because they feared her, but not I. My kindness kept a roof over and food in the belly, because I understood her gift more than most."

"She had the gift too?" The room felt smaller. The books, so full of knowledge, but empty of the facts of it all.

"Hush now, girl. Listen." Mama flattened out her apron before continuing. 'Small things at first, but I had a keen eye from the start and I gave aid to her skill. Yes, she had the gift. Unnatural some said, unholy others. Like you, a little of her blood could heal a sickness, take away an infection. How could it be against God's plan. No, a gift from heaven, and that's the word I spread. They requested us in villages other than our own, and even on one occasion visited a city.' The edges of her mouth edged slightly into a shadowed smile, the yellow and black of her teeth visible. "Now that was a grand occasion.'

"I should like to visit a city one day," I interrupted with a yawn. Tiredness overtaking me despite the desire to hear all.

"Stop me again, girl and you'll feel for it, so help me." I opened my mouth to make amends and thought better of it.

"Years passed us by and she ripened into a woman despite not knowing the ups and the downs." She ground her teeth in such a way I sunk back in the chair. Mama's elixir relaxing my muscles into the cushioned cloth. The logs snapped against the flames like the crack of brittle bones, my eyelids full and heavy. When Mama started up again, her voice sounded far away.

"I gave aid to her, helping with her gift, to turn a coin for us both. Just a little blood could do so much, and that got me thinking."

She rested her tea on the table between us and reached out her hand for the book I had balanced on the side of my chair. Instinctively, I reached for it also, my chest pounding. Mama's eyes narrowed into the heavy wrinkles on her cheek as she shook her palm with insistence. I passed it across, my arm shaking with the burden, as though my muscles had shrivelled with age. The long, crimson, tasselled tail of my bookmark draped across my wrist, tickling my skin.

"A bookseller wraps this cover around the bindings, but will never be the story. You understand this?" She held up the book before pulling the dust jacket away. "Amy?" She repeated with insistence.

"Yes, Mama." I said thickly. The edge of Jacob's note slipped from between the folds, it's edge poking out from between the pages as she brandished the book. My eyes widened, my heart plunging deeply.

"The value is in the book and not the protective cover. Booksellers discarded the covers until collectors saw value in keeping them paired. Those collectors, who can pair the two and make it whole again, fetch a keen price. Do you see?" Again, I nodded my head, uninterested by all this talk of booksellers, my focus on the tiny piece of Jacob emerging from the press of pages. At any moment it may fall free and if Mama saw, there would be no chance of meeting. She would not allow it.

"For a long time I considered. Just a thimble of blood saved a life from infection, but what of drinking freely?"

My insides twisted against themselves. Mama's face flickered red with the dancing flames of the fire. She slammed the book against the arm of the chair, making me jump, despite the ache at the back of my eyes.

A coldness swept along my spine, but could do little more than rest my head back into the corner of the arm chair. Mama pulled herself up and walked towards the mantal, picked up the little box which rested there. From inside she pulled a small dagger and walked back to me. The tip gleamed wickedly, the cut I knew well.

"An old woman, back then. Too old to keep an eye, as I should have. She betrayed me, your mother." My mouth fell open, a whirl inside me as I tried to catch hold of her words. Mama, shook her head and leaned in to my arm. The sharp point of metal resting against my pale skin. "Ay, your mother. I let your mother make her own way of things. Given her all the freedom, and she'd met with a man's promises. No good came of it. A child born. Suddenly life was less." She pressed the point inwards, my arm jerked under her firm grip. The pain nothing more than a pinch, numbed by the liquid which gave a haze to the room and the faint line of red which appeared.

"Yet, I saw something in that child, just as I had done with the mother. The gift passed on and a deal still to be made. As for the mother, she had nothing to offer except a drain on all around her."

Mama pressed her mouth against the white of my wrist and sucked noisily at the blood, her feet spreading with her vigour, knocking the furniture around her. The book slipped to the floor. My tilted head watched Jacob's note fall free. The room whirled around me, faster and faster while Mama fed and all I could think about was Jacob. When she pulled away, red against her lips, her teeth stained as she smiled. The smell of flour so close to me as she breathed.

"Just a sip, before you leave me is all that I need, girl. Just a sip." I could do little more than blink, as she got back to her feet, more nimberly than she had settled. The solid structure in my head sagged at her words. Her foot edging the note under the chair. The white just visible in the shadows. Mama sat back on the chair, moaned with contentment as she always did.

"You still with me, girl? In the blood you see? A spark of extra life for every time I took a little more. But what is extra time if you can't enjoy it with a place to live and food to enjoy. That's the thing of it." She picked up her tea and stirred the spoon. It clinked against the inside of the china. "So a deal done, and time to honour it is here. I had to keep you safe, pure until the time. What else coud be done? Do you see, girl?" My head dropped in a nod. Mama's finger prodded me. "This is the way of it. Always the way."

"The way," I repeated, echoing the circling ideas.

"You need your rest, Amy." The mantel clock clicked agonisingly against numerals as she bent forward, reaching towards the book on the floor, the slip of paper a fingertip away.

"Mama," I blurted out. That name I'd known her by, now empty and worthless. She twisted towards me, the looks I'd mistaken for motherly concern nothing more than malace and greed. I slumped over, falling forwards out of the chair, the room moving around me. Mama watched, looking down on me. She placed the book delicately on the trolly, patting its surface.

"Tonight, we have an engagement. We will attend the Addington Estate. The book needs its cover." She said. A grin revealed the blood stained teeth. Jacob's note slipped its way back into my fist and in turn I pushed it into the folds of my clothes as she pulled me to my feet.

****

I did not know when I woke, except that it was much later than I would typically have napped. My head groggy, throbbing as I edged across the sheets. Candlelight flickered against my dresser, creating endless shadows across the walls. The coarse scent of matches still hung in the stillness. Outside, the leaves collided with each other, an ebbing chorus of voices, just out of my understanding.

I still wore my day clothes and quickly rummaged in the pocket for Jacob's message. My fingers pressing into one corner and then the next.

There it sat. The tiny creases filling me with hope.

Disappearing back into the pillow, I lingered on the edge of sleep once again, until I noticed the moon crescent through the window. I feel the urgency of needing to be elsewhere and yet I'm uncertain.

My first steps out of bed, clumsy and fragile. No doubt, her elixir had done this work. I stall at the door. A dress, the shade of midnight, hung from the hook normally reserved for my cloak. I'd never seen it before. The richness across its dark folds and the elegant filigree made me want to touch the fabric. I glided over and yet never seemed to reach it. She must have slipped inside at some point because the next she was helping me remove my tunic, tightening the bindings across my chest and back to hide my shame; the new finery sliding across my skin.

"Is this mine?" I asked. She only nods, her blue gaze against my own, hands pressing hard against both sides of my face. Tears sparkled like diamonds at the corner of her eyes. I wanted it to be pride.

"It is time," she said.

She led me through the house, pushing me in the back when I stall, guiding me through the doorways. I noticed she was naked under her white robe. Her pendulous breasts drooping freely as she twisted around a corner. She had pulled back her hair from its usual curls, slicked back with a dark substance which shimmered in the candles around the house. It made her look younger, half her age. I'm not sure how I hadn't noticed these things earlier, when she had first entered my room, except maybe I did. Only my mind had confused the logic.

On the road, next to our cottage a black carriage waited. Two horses, the same I'd seen at the funeral procession, held in perfect stillness, while all around the village had gathered. They stood in rows of white, like lines of unlit candles. A hand guided me inside, my legs fragile like sticks and then the snap of the reigns, the gentle rocking, the leather seats creaking, my body pooling into the glass window. Despite myself, a bursting sensation brimmed around my edges at finally being without her guidance. She gathers to join the crowd behind the carriage and yet this is not the reason my stomach churns. I search the faces of those gathered and yet can't see, head aching with the effort, the carriage gaining speed.

The gates of the church were open, a gaping mouth monstrous, reaching above my transport and out of view, stretching behind into the crowd of white figures and darkness which followed. The vehicle stopped at the entrance to the church. The village flood through the wide stone arch, flowing as one, like a flexing spine. Music starts, an organ I'd only heard from a distance, never being allowed to enter before.

Somebody pulls the carriage door open and drags my arm to the church entrance where I gaze at it's grandness, a nobody presenting herself to the power. Windows of stain glass, carvings of stone and candles, so many candles burning with a radiance. The pews full. Some villagers kneeled, others sat, of all different shapes and sizes, hidden under a mismatch of bleached coverings. None of them turned. Ahead of them all, lay a coffin and next to this Old Mid Addington, her withered form tiny on a large thrown of carved oak.

A blow to the back of my neck sent me forwards, feet tumbling over one another. I looked from side to side searching in amongst the crowds. Many bent low, the rustle of their shrouds, a whispered prayer as I passed, their eyes refused to meet my own, instead locking onto the tiny details ahead of them.

The music halted abruptly as I reached the end of the alter. The woman, I'd known as Mama stepped forward, not even glancing at me. When she spoke, her voice was clear and loud, echoing against the corners of the church.

"As you know, Lady Addington has provided us with safety and reassurance in a time of war an unease. We have all benefited from her benevolence. It is her will, we use the blood promised to her, to heal the weak and sick of this village. It is her will which allows me to treat the infections and illnesses which plague the rest of humanity. We gather here today, to repay our debt to her. To give her our offering, so she can continue on with renewed vigour."

Another shove sends me forward, my feet tripping up first one step and then the next. The casket open to my side. Pale face, dark skin around the closed eyelids, of Rev Micheal inside.

27

"We have two choices as you see before you today. Our dear Rev. can do no more good in this world while Lady Addington still has an opportunity."

I'm next to Lady Addington, her neck as thin as chord, her skin a mask over bone, which struggles to turn. I'm pushed to my knees, my whole arm laide bare. A cushioned knife clutched in another's hands. The blade lifted. The edge slices deeply, too deeply to make sense of. The surge of crimson, dripping across the stone, the black dress of the throned woman. Lady Addington opens her mouth revealing teeth like the decaying tombstones of the surrounding graveyard. So much time had already worn at them, what would more do?

I struggle but another grip holds me fast and my arm is pressed deep into her open mouth.

At first, the head rocks limply against my wrist, blood spilling wildly and then her grip tightens, her mouth clamping into my skin, her fingers digging into me. Still I can't move, pull away. Darkness fills the corners of my vision.

"Stop, please." My voice had no strength. Lady Addington drags me closer, I'm too weak to resist. Falling against her as she drinks deeply. No longer a skeleton in her death shroud but of greater substance. My heart falters, I know I'm growing weak, my life being drained away.

"Leave her," A voice calls. It is a young man, he stands holding a tall candle holder, the tip ablaze with flames. "A life for a life, is not a trade of God!" He has emerged from the congregation, his white robe falling free from his shoulder, the wispy hairs on his chin poke out as he thrusts the metal at others who try and restrain him. Jacob! More than one cry as flames leap up and a sudden heat as some of those in white try and pull free, fire racing across their clothing. The flames leapt across tapestries, and into the air above us and still Lady Addington fed, her body pressing down over my slumped body.

Without warning, I slipped from underneath her, Jacob's arms around me. Lady Addington snarled up at us, more like a wild beast than a woman. Her face smeared, marbled eyes wide with contrast.

"We must run!" Jacob said. The heat of hell upon us as we struggled through the wildness of the flames.

The next I remember is the church from afar, flickering in reds and oranges against the black of the sky. Even from this distance, the heat clung to my face like a mask pressed against my skin. Jacob turned to me, he was no longer a boy but a man. His shoulders back, his head high and from my position on the grass, where he laid me, I looked up to him. We both heard the cries at the same time, animalistic and yet too human to be a beast. Another answered. Whatever had happened, this was just the beginning.

Jacob bent down to look at my wounds, the blood had stopped at my wrist.

"Impossible." He murmured, the orange from the fire below catching only half his face as his eyes darted towards me. The same wild look he had given Mama in the church, he held towards me.

"Jacob…" I began, but knew there would be nothing I could say which change the way he thought. If I was to remain by his side, like Mama's then it would all begin again and I couldn't do this. I pushed him back more forcibly than I had meant to. He fell at my feet. I stretched myself out, arms and my blue dress ripped acorss my back revealing the wings, i'd kept hidden for so long, barely stretched. Now it was time for them to be seen.

Jacob, backed away from me whispering a prayer of some description. He held on to the wooden cross he had whittled himself. The look in his eyes changed everything. There could be no between us now, no understanding. He would only replace Mama, in one way or another.

Another monstrous scream came from somewhere in the village. The fire seemed to be spreading. A cry responded to it.

"What's happening Amy? Is it punishment? What have I done?"

"I don't know, Jacob. You should go. Get out of these parts and never come back" I felt the menace inside me and wondered if he could understand the subtle shift too.
He stumbled to his feet.

"I'll go my own way." I'd like to say I flexed my wings and gracefully took flight above Jacob, above all of them, but I'd not mastered any of those skills. Instead I turned by back on him, the church, the village and walked down the hillside, away from the secrets I'd known for my whole life. Whatever Jacob did, was no longer my concern. Whatever the villages did, was no longer my concern. If Mama lived or died, it mattered not.

My journey had just begun.

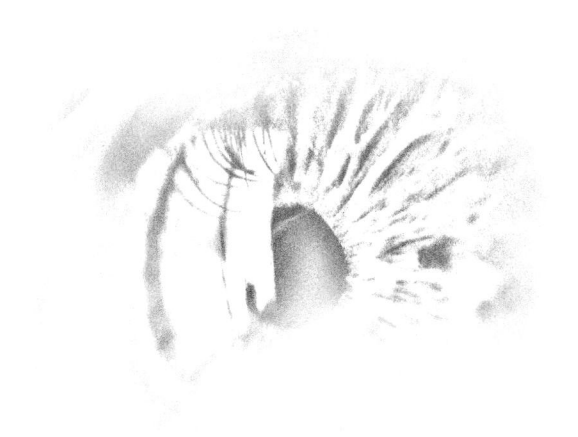

THE HOUSE WITH THREE WALLS

Maybe he had made mistakes, but did he deserve this?

"Thomas Sinclair-Jones," his lips cracked like dried wood. It took a moment to find the right way to move. His joints sore from the cold now he no longer had anything to wrap himself in.

He manoeuvred his head to see around the gloom of the large first floor room. The only light crawled its way sickeningly over the top of the staircase barely able to catch any of what may lie in wait for him in the darkened corners. Propped up on his arm, he stared into the inky blackness until it became a part of him and certainty took hold. Alone, none of her gifts waited for him.

That's how it had been for the first few days, if days even existed anymore. He woke up crumpled on the floor without understanding that first time. Wondering from one sparse windowless room to the next in search of an answer. The house, filled with a lack of furniture, rundown, so far removed from what he knew. It must have been a cruel trick. Gone were the chandeliers, the rich carpets and portraits he had spent a lifetime curating. Instead, simply painted walls and a vast emptiness occupied each space, with the bare minimum of of comfort, until it didn't.

He got to his feet, unsteady, still weary of the corners, and the floor for what she may have left behind and he may have missed through the squinting and blurriness of it all. His heart pounded impossibly in the emptiness. The walls, the wardrobe and the bed were all still in place as he stumbled towards the top of the staircase. His, the only movement, and yet he couldn't help the needling of piercing eyes creep into his imagination.

Despite himself, he paused on the top run. The staircase dropped steeply down to the hallway below. It creaked as he shifted his weight. Scuff marks of the oversized boots she had given him still rested in thick black lines on the wall where he pushed himself over the banister. The runs in the stairway leaned outward like the broken rib cage of an animal. The sheet snapping them and not his neck as it took his weight.

It wasn't this that held him in place. The remembrance of his attempted leap of escape still gave him hope, some control against her. It was the partially open wardrobe, which made him turn.

With each step slower than the last, he edged back into the room. The back of his heel burned from rawness as the crude leather ripped at his skin and yet the floor was worse. Rough timber, embedded grains of wood on the pads of his foot as he had dashed around, in the beginning. Now he fought the dizziness, the tight grip of hunger in his stomach, the voices of the past which plagued every deafening roar of emptiness.

Another step, closer to the certainty of what he had seen poking through the partially open wardrobe door.

He knew every room. Searched every space and beat every wall in the house, certain he would find a way out. That's what he did. How he had carved a success, finding ways when others couldn't.

The vast coldness of the upper floor contained only a bed. She must have removed the ripped sheets he had fastened into a noose. The empty wardrobe had materialised with a sudden clatter catching him off guard.

Yet the closer he got to the wardrobe, the more he was certain that the partially open door had a piece of fabric caught in place.

"Thomas Sinclair-Jones" His throat burned with thirst, and the countless unanswered cries, and the reminder of the noose, although no longer there, still tight around his neck.

His arm trembled as he reached out to the handle. The hinges screamed in pain as metal scraped against metal. The fabric, edged in lace, fluttered and fell back into the crevice of solid darkness as if pulled back out of reach.

He knew it was clothing belonging to someone other than him. Ice fingers clawed the back of his neck as he inched open the door. Preparing himself for the contorted form he knew must lurk somewhere. With a final pull, he revealed the interior, unable to breathe, or move or cry at the contents.

When he opened his eyes in the house, a little hope always clawed its way back with him. Memories of the man he knew, more real than the stale squeeze of the surrounding walls. The longer he scratched away at the house, moving mindlessly from room to room, the less of him remained, like water eroding soil from the edge of a stream, until nothing remained of the curves of his life.

Caught by the movement of the wardrobe door, the row of clothes shuddered on the rail, like terrified children huddled together. Some draped the bottom, rustling as he reached in. Others hid themselves, lost amongst the folds.

He pulled at the first, a dress so familiar against his fingertips. A stain, ragged and dark around the neck. Snatching it, he pressed it against his face. The smell, a morning meadow, stables, the parlour fire crackling with burning oak, hung to the fabric. Whether it was there, he inhaled as deeply as he could. His heart a snapped string, although he already knew. She had shown him Edith, or what Edith had become. Its twisted, broken shape lying abandoned, the last he woke. Certainly it remained in wait for him somewhere in the house.

Moving from one garment to the next and the next and the next, he slid them across in a frenzy. Some worn and faded, others fresh, flashed in front of him. Shirts too coarse to be his own. A boys school uniform, an aged coat belonging to another era. He moved on, not daring to consider who they belonged to, only that they weren't Alegra's.

When he got to the last, he held onto it, his grip tightening on the shoulders where the thin wire hanger gave it some shape. If Thomas could have cried, he would. But there was no moisture left. Only raw pain at the back of his eyes. He tightened his hands into fists, tearing at the workman's overalls that could never have been Alegra's as something sharp and wicked pierced his skin.

Alegra always made the worst of the world fall away. Her boarding bag still unpacked on the polished marble, face upturned so pleased to see him. Thomas Sinclair-Jones' fears fell away with that deep embrace. Edith glowed with pride as Alegra spoke. How she had missed them all entwined with the plans for the winter break in quick bursts of energy. If his hand shook as he poured another red, they didn't notice. Thomas kept the business separate. Allegra had always gotten what she had wanted; she was not to understand. Besides, there were other cutbacks which could be made. Ways to keep them secure. He always found a way.

Pulling back, he dropped the overalls and snatched the hanger. One of the folds of wire had come loose, sticking him in the wrist with its ragged edge. Thomas examined the point, uncurling the rigid shape with his boney fingers to form a thin malleable strip of steel.

"Thomas Sinclair-Jones," he repeated with each bend of the wire.

A loud, sudden scrapping of wood, like cumbersome furniture being dragged across the flooring, halted his progress. That's how it happened in the house. Sounds caught up with him, after he woke, like part of his captor's movements lingered after she left.

He limped to the edge of the stairway once again, wire clutched in his hand. The hallway below had two openings leading into the only other rooms in the house. Light spilled from each room, touching the hallway. Fading as it struggled its way towards Thomas.

Laughter, like tiny silver bells, gently entwined the stillness. Then the tips of his boots against each step of his descent. Watchful, against the shiver of light. A sudden movement in the room unseen. He paused. Working his jaw, hesitant to call out, knowing he would be at the threshold soon enough. Whatever waited Thomas, it couldn't be changed by a cry, or a moan, or a wish.

Once in the hall, he moved to the door on the left. A single bulb hanging from the ceiling, the threads of the rug poking upwards like weeds, the small kitchenette with dry taps and empty cupboards. How many times had he searched, hoped for it to be full, half full, have something to nourish him? That tap, a swan head dipped into a dry basin, it was always dry. No connections, no splash of liquid which he could press into, lick at, savour.

Nothing.

To his right, the light dimmed and ignited as if the shimmering gold had been cased and set free. The sound of porcelain against a table, of cutlery being laid. Intrusive, fading into insignificance at the very same moment.

He spun around. Too quickly to keep his balance without support. His body ached with mistreatment. No doubt, the bruises rising like damp around his waist. Legs of rubber, his abdomen jolting with each jerking footfall as he moved to the last room of the house. Thomas' body rested before the opening, knowing that he would enter and what he might see there. There was no place to hide, not like before.

Alegra had looked panicked, returning upstairs twice, thrice, stopping her before it became too much of delay. Rawness pooled under Edith's eyes, stretching the pigments of her skin. Thomas rested his back to the door, pushing away the crowds, the flickerty flick of cameras and the cry of anguish which plagued their every outing. Finally Alegra returned. Thomas pushed himself away from the doorframe and took them both in his arms, swiftly in the carriage, as it pitched and bounced with each slash of the whip. The gates slid open and the placards, shouts and flash of burned images stunned his eyes.

"Look to your book Alegra. Your book," he said, while shaking the width of his newspaper. Edith glanced into the crowd, the faces stretched with rage. "Pay no mind, aid her with her book will you." He shook out the pressed pages again, paper caught in wind. The front sheet he ignored, folding it away. None of it mattered. He carried no blame. He was as much a victim of the times as anyone of the ebbing mob that held their position as the horses clawed, the coachman cried and the carriage shouldered its way through.

Despite the stamped fresh sting of ink pressed to the thin parchment, he too glimpsed the raging fury of the workers. Not just the men he may have passed in amongst the heat and rage of the factory floor, but also the wives bent over with tears. The young boys, old enough to earn their future. The girl with her ganguly dolls, still caught in the fantasy of childhood. Then like a falling star, licked with the movement of fire he saw it arch towards the carriage. The sudden tearing of air, whooched out and engulfed with embers of crumbling parchment ahead of Thomas. A shudder, a tare, a whinny of horses and the upsurge of calls as he battled against the engulfing flames.

Another noise, like the clinking of cutlery against crockery, drove him even closer. Breathless, he waited. The corner of the poorly constructed table in view. The varnish peeling and blistering.

Another step tearing at the illformed scabs of his heel.
"This is not my house."
Breathless, he plunged into the room. They waited for him.

The brightness stung at his glassy eyes, like needles sewing them into place. Thomas stalled, his legs failing him at the sight. The little beat left in his heart stumbled painfully, hardly believing the terrifying vision in front of him.

She had set the table for three, with cutlery gleaming in rows of silver and plates of white porcelain ready. Scraps of cloth, meant to resemble napkins, folded into neat squares, their edges poking out from under beakers. A candelabra, nestled in between jugs and assorted serving bowls, lids covering what lay inside.

He covered his mouth.

Their backs to him, two people sat at the table. An adult on the left and a child on the right. Neither of them moved, their arms resting on the table in front of them. The bodies stiff and unnatural, forced into position. Both stared out in front of them. The adult's hair, speckled with grey and wiry, combed impossibly out of shape so that it circled its head like a dark halo. The girl's once long hair, now gone. Cut carelessly and pulled, leaving the white dome, like cracked porcelain showing through against the strands. Their dresses hung loosely from their frames, but he knew the items of clothing well.

Thomas wanted to run, to scream, to cry, but could do none of these things. Instead, he stepped closer, his shoes clunking on the floor. He had to see what she had done to his family.

Hesitantly, he nudged the shoulder of his wife. The head lolled, falling forward as if in preyer before the body collapsed over to the side of the chair and into Thomas' outstretched arms. Edith's body no heavier than the fabric which contained her as he brought her down to the floor and turned her over.

Edith's face was not her own. She had no mouth or nose and only pinpricks of eyes cast into the rubbery dome. When he pressed himself into her, he felt only padding where her body should have been, and yet the lingering scent swallowed him.

The face of the other thing, still looked forward across the dining table. It mocked him, his life, his family as its pretence of humanity and he could stand it no longer, whatever the consequences.

He swept at the table and the candlestick at the centre of her arrangement. It bounced away, clearing a path through the tinkling china, sending one then another crashing to the ground. The next he threw it to the wall, while another smashed into the ceiling, showering him with pieces of porcelain. Before he knew it, he had pulled over the laughable interpretation of Allegra, which thudded heavily to the ground. A fire burnt through him with each kick and punch and tear at the thing. The head crunching underfoot until it came free, white chords were all that connected it to its stump. Still, he needed more. The pain of it all unbearable.

A knife from the once carefully arranged dinner display lay next to the battered lump. He snatched at it. The blade too thick against his skin, blunt and useless no matter how hard he pressed. Still, he thrust the solid cold metal forward, stabbing at the air; an illusion barely powerful enough to give him a slither of reassurance of some form of defence against her. He needed it to end.

"I don't belong here. This is not me!"

As if in response, he heard her arrival. The pounding of footsteps, the crash of a door and the silvery bells of her laughter as the front of the house shook. He wobbled back to the hallway, the floor quaking as she entered, but this time he would be ready.

"I'm here," she called. Her childish giggle thundered around him. The house rocked as she scraped at the latch and he swayed with the movement, backing into the shadows as he waited for her to enter, his body rigid.

The wall rumbled, and a slither of light cut through the gloom from the corner. Thomas Sinclair-Jones had his back to the wall. Success or failure, she would not keep him prisoner any longer.

The entire wall swung outwards, hinges squeaking with the effort, floor rolling under him. Her freckled face appeared, grubby stains across her cheeks evident, as she leaned into her doll's house.

"There you are, little man. I hope you're not naughty today. I'm not in the mood." Her voice an avalanche around him. "I've got something for you, if you're good." Her head pressed in against the open wall, her breath sour.

He didn't move. Her eyes loomed closer, nose almost within striking distance.

"Why are you hiding back there?" She pressed in closer.

Thomas' hand tightened around the knife in one hand and the edge of the wire hanger poking free from his sleeve in the other.

"If you're silly today, I won't be happy. I've already said what I'll do. I'll bite and bite until your head pops off." She gnashed her teeth at him. They clamped down like ivory boulders crashing against one another, her gigantic eyes boring into him.

Her eyes, monstrous orbs clicking with moisture, darted to the side.

"You've found my surprise! Do you like it?" She pulled away, leaving the wall in front of him open.

"Look, look I have something for you."

Her face ducked down out of view, leaving tatty blond ringlets bobbing as she worked at something on the ground. Card ripped, plastic rustled as she called up to him.

"You better say thank you. I stole the money from Daddy. He'll be angry when he finds out. Now he's not got a job, he's always angry."

Thomas took in the room beyond. The doll's house elevated; the ground too far to jump without breaking himself. Her bed in the far corner, faded wallpaper across the wall, black mould creeping down from the corner. The curtains drawn, dampening the sunlight. A dresser sat directly opposite, chipped and missing some handles with a lopsided teddy perched on its centre, threadbare patches of fur and a button eye dangling from its socket.

He hurried towards the opening to the house, his feet rested on the edge as he peered down at her. She struggled with the wrappings, her head bowed, the back of her neck visible. Thomas tightened his grip on the makeshift weapons.

Then he noticed the pile of ragged dolls at the foot of the dresser. They lay one on top of the next, their limbs bent, heads twisted unnaturally, cocked backwards in a sightless stare towards the doll's house. So many lifeless faces looking at him, open-mouthed, their last cries frozen in place.

His whole body weakened. He lost his grip on the knife, which tumbled forward, falling noiselessly, swallowed by the carpet below. Thomas lent forward, a moment of weightlessness and it would be over.

"Here you go." Her head loomed back into view. Thomas pulled back as her clenched fist reached towards him, nudging him with her knuckles. The blow sent him sprawling backwards as she opened her fingers, spilling the contents of her hand all around him.

"I hope you're hungry. I have some food for you." She smiled wickedly at him. "I bet you're all hungry!"

A plastic roast chicken lay next to him, badly painted to resemble the real thing. Next to this, a bowl of fruit, misshaped ovals and squares in greens and blues, empty plastic milk bottles painted white, cardboard boxes with pictures of cereal, corn, rice, eggs. Plastic cylinders with paper labels showing baked beans rolled back and forth before settling.

"I got the whole collection. It will look good in the dining room."

"Please." He begged without words or movement.

"Hurry up they're waiting." Her eyebrows furrowed. She reached in and grabbed hold of his leg squeezing so tightly, he could see it compress into nothing against the tips of her monstrous fingers. The pain tore through him. The room span as he was hoisted above the dinner table and crushed into one of the seats. In front of him, the table sat untouched. Alegra and Edith glared at him through the mockery of faces.

"You should say a prayer before you eat." She snapped his head back and forth roughly with her hands. She giggled, the bells echoing through his head. "Now let's get you ready to eat." She bent one arm and then moved to the next. "Ouch." She pulled back, pushing her thumb into her mouth before reaching back in a striking him with the back of her hand. He fell to the ground, his body slumping, his limbs immobile. "You naughty man. What have you done to me?" He heard her sucking at her finger. "Let me loo at you."

She slid him along the floor, his head clattering against the corner of the table.

"Your arm has a wire coming out. Not fair! Your dirty, and broken." She leaned in over him. "I bet I could fix it. That's what I'll do. I'll get my doctor's set. She sounded excited again, enthusiasm bubbling. "That's it. I might have to amputate your arm. I've already practiced with my other dolls. Look. Look."

She held out one of her dolls by the hair. Its head stiff, the rest of the body swayed back and forth, a leg was missing, white thread stained red wrapped around the stump. It dress familiar, a girl's dress he knew. The body plopped next to him on the floor.

"Where is my doctors set?" She closed the front of the house, the little latch clinking shut.

He turned into the dress and the little girl's body. A face he loved, now pale and sunken. The chandelier flickered and faded into darkness.

Outside the house, he could hear her laughing, like the sound of little silver bells.

BOARDWALK

"What a miserable day," I call across the boardwalk to Bernie. Steam pours out of his coffee machine. It smothers his body against the cold for the briefest of moments before dissipating across the counter and the buckets of candy floss, which hang crookedly around the side of the stall.

He is cleaning down. His face still, distant and emotionless against his duties. I try again.

"It's supposed to be the beginning of summer…" Another blast of air froths and sizzles, drowning out my words, although Bernie manages a backwards glance in my direction, communicating everything he needs to in that one gesture. I continued anyway, knowing he probably won't hear. "I'm sure it will be much better tomorrow." Hopefully, I sound optimistic, although I notice his shoulders slump. I wonder if I should keep on talking about the weather, or bring something else up entirely. For a moment, I even consider reminiscing on Jocelyn before the boardwalk took her, but I know Bernie well enough; he wasn't in the mood for stories.

Standing at the other side of the counter, I watch Bernie pull coffee cups from under the serving area, thick plastic wrapping catching against his bent fingers. I make a gesture to help, just as he tears free the disposable containers.

"Tomorrow will be a better day," he says as he stacks the cups next to the coffee machine, ready for tomorrow's customers. He is hopeful, if nothing else. On quiet days, when Bernie has very little to do, his wistful stares focus into the distance, beyond the pier, the horizon of the sea, the clouds, and into a past lingering just for him.

Bernie had never been the same since the boardwalk took Jocelyn. The tattered threads on his yellow collar, the fabric translucent, ripping across the fold, indicating her absence more than any conversation. Bernie turns back to his chrome coffee machine, cloth in hand to give it a final clean. The polished steel, an enormous investment he bought five years ago after the first coffee chain had opened on the High Street. Jocelyn had disagreed. She always disagreed with him. That's what made them an entertaining couple; I'd always loved the playful bickering between the two of them.

"If they serve coffee, we do it better!" He had cocked his head to the side and smiled. She rolled her eyes back at him.
"Fool! My mother always said as much. You weren't the only dessert on the trolly. I had my pick once." The corners of her

mouth gave away her playful intention.

"I knows it, you always tell me about the desserts but now you has the best desserts every day with me. We has the raspberry ripple, the mints, the strawberry, the chocolate fudge, and all the best. I give you the best because you is the best."
"Oh, shut up you old fool. How much is this going to cost us this time?"

"Is not so expensive. In five years, we get ten times what we pay. We get the holidays. We retire. It's so simple." His eyes sparkled, the surrounding lines disappearing to reveal a much younger man.

"How about this year? We never get a break as we are. Are you sure you want to do this, Bernie?"
"Just give me five years."

A deep sigh carries Bernie off into the distance, and with that, my resolve to cheer him. I hope the drizzle will stop, the wind die, and he will at least have a comfortable walk home.
It had happened right here on the boardwalk, her body crumpling across the wood in front of the tourists. Saliva, frothed and white, gathered at the sides of her mouth as her eyes rolled back in her head. Still, the crowd stepped around her, children being pushed to the side by their parents as the circle widened. Bernie had to battle his way through, leaving a queue of impatient customers at the stall.

I didn't know how to help her, how to get her lungs working again or do anything to keep her alive. It's then I saw the presence grab up through the boards as though reaching up from the thrashing waves below.

I couldn't let the boardwalk have her completely. "I'm just going to have a last walk around as everybody shuts down for the evening." My voice is little more than a mumble. I don't wait for a response from Bernie.

On a good evening, the pier is open until late, and at the peak of summer, with the late nights, it used to be busy. The fairground is just behind, its flickering lights beautiful against the laughter of young crowds, new romances, and old romantics. It is all there for me as I patrol. Recently, however, the curse of this place has grown. Like a menace from a fairy tale, I see it. Shades of absence, dragging at any life it finds, hungry for those that linger, so nobody does.

Bernie is oblivious to the danger, but I'm always on my guard, ready for the beast to emerge. How I hate the pier, knowing this evil has it in for me, too.

Although I shouldn't give myself over to it, not even for a moment, I do so anyway, pausing in the centre. Out towards the horizon, the clouds edged in grey and then disappear leaving a patch of clear early evening sky. Eventually, the dismal weather shall pass, but for now, it continues, flicking in from across the sea in a harsh spray. I can remember that numbing cold across my cheeks, enough to give a tiny taste of being alive. I clench myself tightly, stamping with sudden energy.

Rows of Victorian lamp posts protrude in perfect symmetry along the boardwalk, continuing towards the end of the pier. In between each one, a rain-drenched bench painted in black gloss gazes out past the iron railing to the views beyond. In all the years I'd been here, so much care had been taken to preserve the boardwalk, keeping the past part of the now, as though there was some value in the things that have happened before us. All they had created was a monster, a predator lurking undetected by most. The panels of wood flooring shimmered with the watery coating, like the scales of a snake lying in wait for its prey. The churning waves, it's hiss, attempted to pull me onwards towards the end of the pier, but as always I resist. I turn back to Bernie, not wanting to leave my only connection alone with the beast.

I'd found that the answer was to keep moving. I've little choice in the matter. My restlessness is for a good reason. If I wait around for too long, the boardwalk's greed will absorb me too. Most of the time, it's only little pieces torn from me, although who knows what this monster may take next.

Bernie doesn't say anything as I return. Instead, he looks right at me with wide eyes before quickly flicking on the lights at his stall again. They spark into existence, highlighting the gloomy evening. The little bulbs chase each other around the opening in his kiosk repeatedly. Confusion washes over me. I show as much, but his attention drifts past me, as though I'm not there.

I notice them too now. A crowd of people gathered at the entrance to the pier, all of them damp, many chatting in quick excited tones.

"What is this?" Beanie says. This time I struggle to respond as the crowd moves towards us.

"This way now." A short woman with an enormous umbrella emerges from the group as they part to let her through. "An opportunity for refreshments," she calls into the crowd while pointing towards the twinkling lights of Bernie's stall. "David, get the equipment," she says into the darkness beyond the steps.

Before I know it, they are pushing me aside to form a large queue. I don't resist, just move into the background.

"You are still open, I take it?" The short woman says to Bernie, not giving him time to answer before they attack him with the first order. The coffee machine pumps and slurps, as one after another from the queue step to the side, hands warming around their coffee. "As predicted, the drizzle is dying away." The woman shakes the umbrella, sending a spray of water at an even shorter, and very round man. He doesn't react; he is too busy struggling to unburden himself of several large holdalls strapped around his body. Perspiration covers his face from the effort. Despite having not left the pier for some time, I knew the nearest road is quite a distance and imagined the effort of it all. "We shall begin. David, we'll need the K-2 and the cameras ready to go."

Before Bernie's stall, Norman and Ada's fish and chips stood in this place. Typically, crowds flocked around on a Friday or Saturday night while music played. Most of the time, there was no trouble. These are the little things I can hold on to. If there is some connection that sticks, then I can keep it with me. That's how I know time is moving forward; otherwise, I am lost. In this case, the folded newspaper packaging, hot, torn at the corners, held itself in my memory. It wasn't a fondness. Instead, it was a torturous experience in which it didn't matter how close I got. When I observed the tiny white grains of salt across the broadside of fried potato, damp with vinegar, I realised there was no scent. Not only this, my realisation was like a blow knocking me off balance. I would never taste or touch again. As ridiculous as it is, chips made me realise the things I'd left behind, even if I couldn't remember why I wanted them back.

In those days, there was less urgency; it didn't want me as much. I could lie on the benches and lose myself in the loneliness of nights. Or maybe it wasn't that long ago after all. My memory is thin, bent over in places, twisted, so the end meets the beginning like the grease-covered chip wrappings. Perhaps the beast devoured my memories first, pulling them into her foundations to digest. This pier takes so much from me with every opportunity. On those busy days, when the world was awash with movement and colour, I wondered why I'm here. Now, it doesn't matter; I have Bernie to keep safe. Visitors peer out to the vastness of the ocean, with glossy dreaming eyes, while I can only ache at the motion of the sea crashing like an eternal clock. I'm nothing more than a dried-out husk of a sea creature washed up against the rocks.

After a short time, Bernie has provided almost everybody with their beverages. The little woman grabs at the opportunity to move in. I'd kept myself at a distance until I see her make a move towards Bernie.

"I will say now, I'm not a coffee drinker, but after being here just a short time, I know I'll be needing it tonight. One coffee, please." The woman looks across at David. He smiles and nods. "Very well, it's just the one. David is fine for refreshment." The small man wipes his brow, his lips droop with a comic elegance before returning to the equipment. "You are?" The woman probes Bernie as though she has only just paid attention to the man behind the stall. Bernie pauses for a moment.

"Bernie," he says. She looks at him, waiting while he scratches his nose.
"I am Madame Espirit." She raises her hands theatrically. Bernie attempts to repeat the words like he is chewing a toffee. Madame Espirit ignores his pronunciation.

"Do you mind if we record you? Just for our subscribers."
Bernie Straightens himself.

"Is for the TV?"

"Oh no Bernie, we have a bigger following on the internet these days. I'm sure you've heard of it, the internet. It would help with our investigation."

"What kinds of investigations with such a big group?"

He scratches the bald dome of his head.

"You are a wise man, Bernie. Well, I will be brief, as I will address the group shortly." Bernie nodded. "The paranormal!"

My dislike of the woman crystallises. The problem with these types is they see what they want to see. If people want to believe something, it doesn't matter what evidence there is, they will believe. People like this lookout for the vulnerabilities in others, they suggest there is a dark figure under an arch, and everybody thinks there is. Even if nobody can identify the dark figure, it's there because they want it to be. I've seen so many of her type on the pier. The fortune tellers and mediums conducting their stupid performances in little tents. I've listened to them all.

"Are you aware of a presence here, Barry?" Her eyes drink in Bernie. He shuffles behind his kiosk, not correcting her.

"His name is Bernie!" I hiss.

The fraud of a woman holds up her palm as if she has located a draft. "You've lost somebody close to you. I can sense that, Barry. Was it a loved one?" Bernie nods his head, eyes widening. "I can perceive a forceful presence around you."

"My wife, she died here." He leans forward, hands shaking as he rests against the counter. "Is she safe?"

"It is your wife. I can sense her." Madame Espirit places the tips of her fingers against her temple. Some of the group who are close enough to hear, press in. "Your wife's name, it's a beautiful name, it begins with an A?" Bernie shakes his head. "It's a D!" She knits her brow with concentration.

"Her name is Jocelyn," Bernie says. Her name animates his face. "She's with me always."

"Yes, Jocelyn, that's it. She is here!"

"Yes," Bernie says, "Is safe?"

"She is, Barry." Madame Espirit releases the pressure against her head, letting her hands fall to her sides. Her shoulders slump. The people around them attempt to applaud while still clutching cups, a muffled shudder of appreciation. Madame Espirit makes a small bow.

"This form of direct contact is so tiring. It takes so much energy to make that level of connection."

"Jocelyn is still here?" Bernie whispers across to her from the opening of his booth.

"Take my card." A white business card slides from her hand across the countertop before she turns, leaving Bernie staring down onto its printed surface.

I'm shaking, heat rising from the centre of my being. I want to throw myself at her, to scream into her face.

"Throw it at her, Bernie. She can't bring back the dead; she'll do anything to get your money," I say. Bernie picks up the card, anyway. So I turn my attention back to the old fraud. Only she has stopped, her fingers against the side of her head again. She turns and looks at me. I feel coldness, like icy fingers racking through my core as we stare at each other.

"David." Her voice snaps through the air. Everybody jumps, especially the short round man, who is by her side in an instant. "We will begin, let's gather everybody." She rubs her forehead. "And get me one of those." She points at me. Her finger probes beyond to a tub of candy floss hanging from Bernie's stall.

"I've got a terrible headache. I need sugar."

By the time they gather around Madame Espirit, the rain has stopped completely, and the wind has relented. I circle, trying to catch sight of the equipment being unloaded by David through the gaps. Madame Espirit raises her hands until the excited chatter quietens and then fades into silence.

"We are here to find the abandoned, the ghosts who walk among us. With our energy, we can call forth those whom cannot move on and are still part of this boardwalk. Some may choose a location to hold on to before passing onto the beyond, while others are less fortunate. The K-2 David has in his hand, allows us to sweep the area for spikes, it channels frequencies beyond our own. Using the K-2 will also detect electronic voice phenomena and allow us, to an extent, have contact with the dead."

"Will we talk to spirits, y'know, like a conversation and that?" A tall lady with heavily dyed blond hair calls thickly from in between chews of her gum. Madame Espirit's eyelids flutter like someone had complimented her on her beauty.

"No. As an individual, you could never commune with the dead, but you must remember I have a gift. Ever since I was a young girl, I've been able to commune with those poor souls who have lost their way." She pauses, looking wistfully to the end of the pier. We all follow her gaze. She even has me caught up in her deception. "Difficulties arise when we invite spirits in. I can negotiate the in-between better than anybody. Some of you have already witnessed this tonight." At this, excited whispers form. Madame Espirit raises her hands again. "We may need to use many techniques to communicate, Oujia boards, trigger objects, and we have modern technology to aid us. Whatever method we use to talk to those that are not of this world, we must remember two things."

I had to get away from her babbling. Turning to walk

back to Bernie's kiosk, hoping for the firmness of familiarity, it stunned me to witness Bernie scurrying towards the group, his face alert, eyes focusing on Madame Espirit.

"Don't listen to her, Bernie! Nothing she says makes any sense," I say, but he walks past me without the slightest acknowledgement.

"The first thing to remember is that when we are to commune with the other side, it can be a confusing fuddle. Remember, there is no flesh and blood, no brain, no chemical synapses to help neurons communicate. Therefore, for the deceased, everything can be a bit of a mess." A murmur ran through the crowd. Madame Esprit raised her voice. "Secondly, some of what lies on the other side can be malignant, hateful, seeking to destroy what it does not have. In other cases, there is just confusion, although the outcome may be the same. The spirit may not be aware of the malign impact it has on the surrounding living. We must be careful."

An older lady at the front grabs hold of the man next to her. He whispers something into her ear. The older lady looks pale. Madame Espirit's speech has done the trick. If I could reach out to her and throttle her, I would.

"Now, we begin. David, the K-2 please." The little man holds up the device. It was the first time I'd seen the thing and almost guffawed at the sight. The small black box looks just like a wireless, only shiny and covered in flashing gages. A long metal antenna stands out from the pack, resting against the man's shoulder. "If you are here, speak to us. Use our energy. Say your name."

A silence follows. Only the sound of the waves at the end of the pier interrupts the vacancy. They crash and pull against the sand, and the wooden piles embedded deep into the ground.

We listen.

"David!" Heads jerk. The whites of David's eyes grow large. "The volume, if your wouldn't mind!"

Muted laughter spreads across her followers, easing the tension so tangible in the surrounding air. David juggles the device, his chubby fingers twisting a dial until static erupts from the electrics.

"Let us start again." Once more, she places her fingers against the temples of her head, a strand of hair dangles from the tightly wound bunch. "Can you talk to us? Who are you?"

Static continues to fall from the device; its smashed streams of hissing colliding within itself. The old lady at the front grips her acquaintance so tightly, the white bone of her knuckles become visible.

"Weather." A distorted voice from the device calls out.
The group looks at each other while Madame Espirit closes her eyes, pressing those fingers deeper into the skin on the side of her face.

"Weather." A few of her followers mouth to each other.
"Who are you? What do you want?" Madame Espirit calls into the crackling electrical pulses. "Speak to us."

"Miserable." The static crackles. "Summer."
"Are you unhappy? We can help." Madame Espirit throws her head back to look towards the darkened sky. "Your name?"
"Beginning. Better. Tomorrow."

By now, her followers are chattering.

"Wait!" the electronic voice calls.

Bernie has squeezed in closer to listen, while I'm beyond caring any longer. I move, but a sinking grabs at me. Stupidity has made me careless. I've lingered too long, and the boardwalk drags at me again. I strain against the fibres of wood with everything I have, pulling, tearing myself free.

"Do you believe it will be better tomorrow? Are you suffering?" Espirit calls while I reach inside myself to separate from the monstrosity of the pier. My freedom is at a price. A piece of me rips. "What is your name? Show yourself? Be here for us." Her voice shrieks, but I'm moving away, not caught by the creature any more.

I'm not sure if she reacts first, or I do. Either way, we both follow the movement. It dashes down the side of the pier, a flurry of red streaming through the darkness like a wound carved into skin. We both watch before the boardwalk consumes the vision in thickening darkness.

"There is a presence. We must move!" Esprit says.

"I sense it too," another voice calls while other faces blink blindly at each other, some open-mouthed. A man rubs the back of his thick neck. The blonde lets out a subdued cry. Bernie is hurrying back to his booth. I'm moving away, towards the apparition. I must know if there is another.
"Bring the K-2," Espirit says.

I continue towards the end of the pier where most of the beast's power resides. To my left, the rusted metal shutter of the deckchair station shakes against the breeze, a bleeding tooth in the mouth of a devil. In the heart of winter, its shaking roar against the wind is my only companion. Even Bernie packs away for a few months each year.

Beneath me, through the spaces in the wood, the dark shadows of sand pass into waves. It moves from stillness to anger in an instant, churning inside me with something like emotion. As the wind picks up, another part of me gives to its grasp. There was so much of myself spread across every surface; it is challenging to keep any presence at all. Still, I push on.

At first there is nothing to see, but the closer I get to the end railing, the clearer it becomes. There is a shape outlined against the horizon. The small form moves, writhing against the bars, unnatural, contorted limbs, arms reaching down into the black noise below, legs dangling against the air.

I don't continue. A flickering inside, like a moth trapped against darkened glass, fills me.

Its coat catches opening suddenly, dark hair stretching around her head, and then a face. A child peers back at me, pale skin, eyes full of fear.

"Wait!" I call, dashing to grab hold of her. "Child!" I'm almost within reach. Her cheeks glisten with tears. "Don't climb. You'll fall. The pain can't be much." Her face sags, salt water against her cheeks. Her head falls forward over the Victorian iron barrier. Legs higher than the railings. There is just the pink of her hand against the darkness. It's the last part of her, holding on to the metal bar before she disappears below.

"No!" My scream is a distorted crackle, chocking in static of the fancy wireless the little round man has lumbered towards the end of the pier.

Espirt's group gathers around me. One or two lean over the railing to gawp into the churning sea below. A foaming mass of dirty bubbles fight as wave after wave crashes against the thick piles whose tips plunge deep below the water, sinking deeper than imaginable. The sea hammers anything caught here against the foundations, thrown into the wood and stone with little effort until the beast breaks it into pieces. I imagine the saltwater in my mouth, sharp against my tongue, biting the back of my throat. It makes me shake or want to pull away, but I can't. I sense the surrounding space. My hands are no longer my own; they have become part of the iron. I tear myself back, desperate to be free.

"Is there a ghost?" One of the group asks.

"You heard the spirit speaker thing. There's a child." The tall lady says, the whites of her teeth on show as she still chews. None of them look at me. I'm nothing but a ghost.

"Do you feel an entity among us?" Espirit calls, her voice warbling pathetically. The group mumble in agreement. They've all made their way here, except Bernie.

Bernie!
It's then I notice it through the gaps of the boardwalk below my feet. A crimson mass presses itself against the wood. I know it to be the beast. Shimmering hollows stare up, just long enough for me to realise the danger, then it hurtles off back towards the stall, the wooden boards hammering as it moves. Bernie is alone back there!

"What's happening?" One of the group yell. Another screams, as the deck vibrates around us.

"Focus your questions on the K-2 ?" Madame Espirit's voice calls from somewhere behind. "David, take over."

That damn woman has woken the beast and now it more aware than ever. I had to protect Bernie, no matter the cost.
I race after the monster, willing to do whatever it takes. Moving with speed is difficult. The beast has absorbed so

much of me; I'm nothing but a partly digested morsel to the monster but yet I keep pace with the shape, as it twists against the underside of the boardwalk in an endless pursuit, meandering, gaining presence as it pulls itself free, squeezing up through the boards, sea water glistening on the red fabric wrapped around its form.

"Can't leave me." The static of the fancy wireless chokes out.

I can't let anything happen to him. He can't leave me.

Bernie is ahead. He's pulled the shutter down in place over the opening in the kiosk, the thick padlock in his hands. He pauses, looks towards the ground as if he notices something below.

I must get to him.

Only between us is Madame Espirit, her hair dishevelled; bonds no longer keep it in place. She pants with effort. Her voice is little more than a whisper when she speaks.

"Many years ago, a distressed, damaged little girl ran from her horrors. Lonely, ashamed, she came here." Esprit takes a deep breath. She raises her eyes, but I'm watching Bernie. He holds out the white business card Espirit had given him before tucking it into his breast pocket. I go to move around Madame Espirit.

'Wait.' She looks directly at me. "She had fought all her brief life. Then one late night it became too much. With nobody to support her, she let go. Her body found, broken and twisted, beneath this pier in 1947."

"What's it saying?" one of her crowd call out. The

voices almost lost in the distance. The static rises and falls.

"It was never her fault, that little girl held no blame."

"You see me?" The wireless crackles.

Bernie walks towards the steps leading to the seafront and away from the pier. I couldn't follow him any more than I could grow wings and fly away, but he will be safe until he opens again tomorrow. No thanks to this woman.
"Nobody could help you then. Let me help you now. Take my hand." Esprit reaches out her hand. It was thin. Tendons prominent through the aged skin.

"You see me?" I say.

"Emily." The crackling voice in the distance calls out.

"You must let the people of this pier go. You must set that man free, Emily."

The name spins wildly around me. So unfamiliar until I repeat it. "Emily," I say.

"Let it all go, Emily."

The pier took Jocelyn. The monster absorbed her after she died. It used her weakness and took part of her away. It happened. This pier has power. It has been hunting me from the beginning and now there isn't much of me left. I couldn't let the same happen to Bernie.

"Can't take him." The distorted voice drifted from the contraption.

"Take my hand, Emily. Let us end this now before there is

anymore harm."

"I care for Bernie. I can't let it take him as well."

"There are many things which none understand. We're not meant to. There is right. There is wrong. There is loss. We see beauty in one day, while the next we do not. When a spirit stays where they are no longer meant to be, they may be around life, but it is not living. They take from the living even if they don't mean to."

On those most glorious days, where there isn't a single cloud in the sky, only the blue from above and seagulls frozen against the breeze, the boardwalk bustles with crowds and colour. I remember the trundling of the carousel, each spin a joy for the children onboard. I take it all in, savouring what is on offer.

"I'll be gone," I say.

"I don't know the truth anymore than you, Emily. It is time for somebody to show you some kindness. Please take my hand. It is time."

"Can you hear me?" I ask. I can't move. How could I against everything I knew, everything I'd forgotten, and yet there was no other choice? Madame Espirit's hair catches on the breeze, and for the first time I can recognise how fragile it was against her skull. She has aged, and yet I know her. She looks down at me. I try to pull back. My feet bury into the bolts, the wood, the dirt of thousands of footsteps. In Espirit's eyes, I can see more than her brown pupils. In the centre, for the first time in so long, set against the canvas of the boardwalk is my reflection. The little girl in red.

"I've felt you from the moment I arrived at this boardwalk. Take my hand." She smiles, a sad movement I've forgotten how to respond to. "It's never been your fault, little one. It's time to say goodbye."

"I'm here." I reach up into her hands only then, realising we've been here before. Thousands of moments slip through me and I study each in turn as I let the boardwalk go.

Against the gathered tourists, there is a young girl. I could see her through the layered bodies like a slither of sunshine on a cloudy day. The familiarity she created cracked through my thoughts, but it's gone before I can keep hold of the memory. Her parents called out through the groups of pier visitors, candy floss toddlers, bulging families, elderly mothers, teens licking ice-cream, and hand in hand couples. Their desperate voices weaved frantically until it pulled my attention, and I could see them. The father's mouth was open, his eyes darted with concern. They pushed through the busy boardwalk. Voices rising in panic. The mother spun on the balls of her feet.

The girl ignores the calls. She focuses on walking in my direction, her fingers pressed against the side of her head. I had nowhere left to go but to the end, where the sea cried out for me. She followed, watching. I reached out.

"Help me," I said. "Take my hand."

The girl's arm lifted towards me. Her tanned skin making the youth of her tiny nails stand out.

"John look!" The mother called. Her father's arms wrapped around her, pulling her away.

"Don't run off again, little Madam." He said as he carried her away.

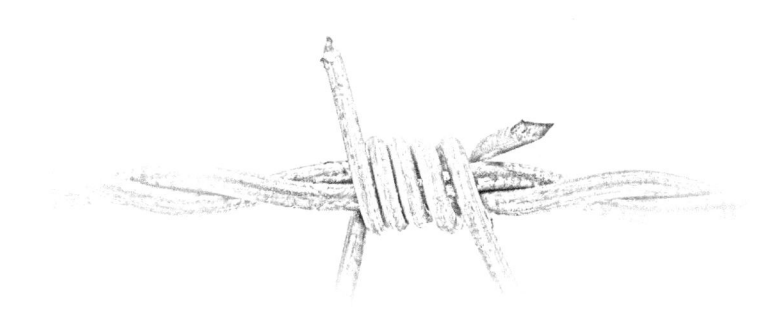

TOMMY

Tommy had tried to pay attention to the lectures about the enemy, standing chin to shoulder with the other men, struggling to listen to the horrors without churning inside and battling to control his trembling lip. If only he could crawl back into her arms. Not that he'd admit such a thing, not then, not later, in the mud and filth of it all. She was back in London, no doubt chatting in the factory about her brave sons. His chest swelled at the imaginings. His heart plummeted at the loss she was yet to know. How disappointed would she be when Tommy returned alone? The same look she had given him when his big brother announced he had signed, while he could not.

Tommy thought he had encountered monsters. He had seen them in the gas around him as he fumbled with the cloth of his mask. The faces of his friends twisted in pain, creating creatures he barely knew.

"Don't act so, Tom. Do what I do, when I say and we'll get through this. I got you this far. They'll only notice your different if you act up and then we'll both be in it." He looked down at Tommy, squeezing his shoulder. "Don't talk. Stay close. Do what I tell you." They didn't notice Tommy. The medical rushed along with basic training and somehow he had made it through. Another soldier, with a proud mother at home.

He had time to reflect later, in the best way he could. He sat with the last of his unit, noticing those that were absent more than those that remained, secretly thinking of their cries. Over and over and over, each time an additional detail dragged itself into his recollection, but always there was the same relief. Fastening the stiff fabric around his head and realising he could breathe while they could not. He clenched his fists at this, and realised he still held his mask, that's what they had told him, so that's what he did. Over and over, until his fingers burned with the roughness of it and his face felt at home.

Tommy thought he had witnessed death, as bloodied hands clutched at his own. Bodies pulsing with the last flow of life before skin whitened, lungs gasped, and breathing stopped. Still, they seemed alive, choosing not to speak because of the pain of it all, that's all. Blood covered his uniform, although the bullets had avoided ripping into his face or digging into his chest. They dragged him away from his brother that day. They had known all along Tommy shouldn't be there, but what did it matter?

As he sat on his own, other units walking past, each crackle of gravel became distant gunfire. His nails dug into his palms at this until his blood did flow. Sleep was impossible. That was when the worst of the beasts arrived.

As a young boy, he was naive to believe he had seen the worst of all there was to see. The cold command of demons and the slaughter by an unseen enemy plagued him, so that black circles formed around his eyes and his skin took on a yellow pallor. The real evil was yet to come.

He had never tried smoking until they attached him to a new unit.

"Sit it out with the Hussars. The dark days are over, my boy. It is only a matter of time now." Commanding voices broadcasted loudly. He held onto their words the best they could, but like his days before all of this, he could only grasp at a few. His big brother had steered him in the right direction. Now he was alone.

The muddy pathways of the trenches eventually led to the Hussars. Tommy reported as he should and took his place amongst the filth. The sergeant looked at him for some time, fixing him with weeping yellow eyes. He tightened shaking hands around his gun until a tall man passed him a cigarette. Tommy hesitated.

"Take it. It's all I've got to give."

"Thank you." Tommy said. He must always remember his manners and his duty. His mother's words, not his own. The spark of a match lit up the face of the man. The flame warmed Tommy briefly as he dragged deeply at the smoke.

"Carlson." The tall man said. "That there is Williams, and that there is Mouth."

Tommy looked at each of the men, repeating the names slowly, but didn't offer up his own. Instead, he let the burning tobacco bite at the back of his throat. Each of the men's face momentarily glowed from a sparking match before the edge of early evening darkness took hold.

The sergeant shrugged. "Well, he has a gun, and he's survived this far." Carlson pressed against the sergeant and muttered something. "Nothing we can do about the boy now," the sergeant said aloud, pushing under water the drowning truth of it all, then turned and walked away, along the carved lines in wet clay.

Carlson watched him go as the rain fell once more. Eventually, he turned back to Tommy.

"It's best we get some rest, in the best way you can. It's busiest here late at night." At Carlson's words, they all slipped back into the crevices they had formed in the trench walls, unable to sit on the ground because of the water pooled around their boots.

"It's been a hard fight around here, kid, the last few days…" Carlson trailed away. "You know… Just be aware, it's starting to smell up there, when the wind changes." Carlson buried himself into his own hollow, only the dim embers of his cigarette visible from time to time.

Tommy didn't try to sleep. The worst beasts came to him when he closed his eyes. Instead, the nicotine kept him company, his mouth numb with poisons as ammunition ran past on makeshift carriers, knocking into those who weren't against the wall. They hurried past Tommy's sluggish gaze, too fast to be men, like huge scurrying rats. Their feet stretched out, bare against the muddy ground, huge toes splayed as claws scratched their way into the mud for purchase. One of them looked at Tommy. It was a face he knew, only now covered in a tight carpet of fur. His brother leaned in, whispery chin hairs touching his cheek. The mouth opened, revealing two long teeth reaching from his top gum.

He woke so suddenly, his hands fumbling with the mask, gasping, tightening against his face. An arm rested on his shoulder.

"It's okay, son. You were sleeping. It was just an ammunition run, that's all."

"Every night's the same. Bloody rat runners!" Mouth pulled himself out of the gloom. "I guess we start then. Getting this place ready for our guests, should they ever decide to drop in?" He pointed to the battleground above. "I'd thought we'd won this war last Thursday!"

"Shut up, Mouth." Carlson said. Another cigarette burned from the corner of his mouth.

Tommy looked back at the rat runners. They were just boys like himself, handing out ammunition as soldiers called for it.

"Looks like there's another push. Another chance to shake our balls at the enemy!" Mouth said.

"Let's hope for just a ration run." Williams said out of the darkness.

"No chance! Not if the ammunition is out. Who's up for a bet it's barb duty?"

Tommy looked at the top of the trench. It was different to the darkness of their pit, instead it was an absence of light pulling back, dragging at them, calling out for their company.
"They can't ask us to go up there, can they." Williams said.
"Some poor fool will have to before daylight." Mouth said.
"I'll do." Tommy said. They couldn't see Carlson shaking his head or Tommy's closed eyes as he spoke.

"I'll do," he said again. Carlson pressed another cigarette

on him, placing it against his lips, but nobody said anything. So when two men were told to go, Tommy did.

He slid himself over the barrier, waiting for the rolled wire to be fed up to him. It's wrapped coils contained against sacking. Carlson followed behind, whispering.

"We have about 40 yards to make before getting to the pickets. The wire's down, so we'll need to run it across. Just stay low and follow me. Do you understand?"

His mother always questioned him so, when she had her tenderness for him.

"You're different, Tommy. You can't do the things that others can. It's your brain. I wish you could understand."

He could carry, and that's what they had asked him to do. He shifted the pack of barb on his back, his body low to the ground, his rifle left behind for the purpose. Tommy nodded, but the nothingness swallowed it whole.

Carlson led the way, keeping low, Tommy scrambling behind across the torn up ground, their bodies low like the cripples who escaped home. Carlson didn't move quickly, instead he considered each moment in stages, before quickly darting in direction, like a rabbit in the fields back home. Tommy stayed close behind. In such darkness, it would be easy to lose sight of him.

They ducked into craters; the edges ragged and unwelcoming, but before long, they encountered the bodies clinging to the surface in their last attempt at defiance. The further they went, the deeper the bodies seemed. Tommy could make out a leg protruding from the side, a boot caked with mud, the laces dangling uselessly, until he peered closer and noticed half a face sandwiched between layers of filth, its single eye missing, skin decomposing across its cheek, so that it grinned with a knowing cunningness which stung acid at the back of his throat. Tommy couldn't take his gaze away from the dead thing until Carlson pushed his head away in the opposite direction with a muddied fist.

"Be all right, lad. Just follow me and keep it quiet. As soon as we make a noise, we're going the same way as that poor soul. You hear me, Son."

They pulled themselves up out of the crater and slithered forward, over broken wood and half buried fragments of metal. All the while Tommy wondered what lay beneath him, deep in the soil, long dead, no doubt. Each pit they tumbled into, he hoped, would be the last, and yet another was just up ahead waiting with open jaws.

"Don't move." Carlson whispered. Tommy tried to stay still, but fell back against the mud, which sucked at his body hungrily. They waited, Carlson low, his head cocked to absorb every sound. The rain pattering against the pools of water around him, the pitter patter of water against metal. He could smell the bodies, ripe decay, clinging against his gums, before the chilling air tugged it in another direction.

Carlson beckoned him towards the lip of the hole. He climbed to the side slowly, reluctantly, fearing what his hands may grab at with each movement. Carlson pointed towards the shapes ahead of them. Bodies draped themselves across the wire, some standing, others on their knees, arms outstretched into impossible positions as if in celebration. Carlson looked away quickly, but not Tommy. The bodies caught ahead of him swayed as the breeze took hold.

"Light," he whispered. "Stay down."

Tommy looked through the dancing bodies and

caught sight of the meagre shimmer in the darkness. It disappeared and then appeared momentarily a little closer to where they were.

"Still." Carlson's voice barely audible, Tommy wondered if had been the wind, but the push on his back forced him closer to the wet dirt until his helmet tilted to the side and his head squeezed against the damp. He listened and in the darkness heard a noise, a gurgle like the sound a plug makes as filth is washed away. He saw the wide eyes of Carlson, the as he tried to place the sound and then the rain roared around them, without warning, like the rattling vibration of his mother's factory.

Cold against his face and the back of his neck. His clothes heavy and he wondered if he hadn't become part of the earth, the trenches, the water. Only the heavy beats of his heart, the warm breath on his neck and the hand on his back told him otherwise. In the darkness, he shivered, the water in the ground seeping into his clothes until he could feel his bones against the hollowness of his body. Still, they didn't move until he thought they never would. Tommy closed his eyes against the chill, knowing that he would feel nothing else ever again.

The barb ahead shook, the thin metal strands straining against each other. A click as the wire loosened, and another as the bodies swayed backwards into them. Tommy opened his eyes to see the hands at work clipping at the wire with cutters. Then the lightness against his back as Carlson's hand slipped away.

Tommy held the air in his lungs, drowning in the moment, as he had done before. A face came into view, then another. Two boys, not much older than him, working to cut through the barrier they were there to repair. They had no forked tongue or blackened eyes. Not the monsters of his teachings, just children doing as they had been told.

Tommy felt the nudge of a rifle against his back. It came again, until he rolled over, the roll of repair barb against his rear. Carlson pressed the rifle at him, a finger pressed to his lips, only it was longer and pointed like a devil's claw.

Their plan formed with simple gestures, Tommy left with the gun as a last resort while Carlson would make for the two widening the barb. The knife shook in Carlson's hand as he pointed it towards where Tommy would perch, hidden against corpses and fragments of battle, but when he peered at the boys at work, he knew Carlson would fall before he had made it to them. Even if he wasn't gunned down, they still outnumbered him.

The boys couldn't hear Carlson ready himself, bracing against the mud, his deep intake of air, the whisper of a prayer. Tommy heard, but kept his eye on the length of the gun, aiming at an impossible target he could barely see. His finger arched against the trigger until it didn't exist, only the rain and the metal and the decay. His heart pounded. Only he would know this end, lost amongst the rot.

One boy looked up directly at Tommy. Even at the distance, he could recognise the surprise, the whites of his eyes, the sudden awareness. He felt it too from under him, a rolling ripple of discontent as the ground shifted and mud fell away next to them.

Carlson pointed with his knife at the grey mass seething free, stripped of earth by the rain. It circled them in a huge coil without end like a gigantic worm contracting and shortening to wriggle forward. Tommy focused back on the enemy, only they were gone. The barb sagged under a hole with the cutters hanging, snagged against its mesh, still rocking up and down with invisible hands, working them.

Again, the soil rolled around them, crashing and clinging against Tommy's legs.

"Move, move," Carlson said and yet neither did. The ground did all the work for them, parting, tearing apart with the flesh of something unimaginable breaking through. Carlson's rifle slid from Tommy's grasp, sliding back down into the crater, down, deeper than possible, until it hit the centre of a writhing mass of oily skin, shimmering with water. The gun broke in half against the squeeze before sinking into the churn.

Carlson worked at the ground, pulling himself over the edge, his legs sliding away and out of view. Tommy's feet lost purchase, the barb roll on his back cumbersome, stopping him from turning. The scent of decay overwhelmed him, his brain fogged with the smell of death being set free from the whirlpool of movement below. He slipped. Another foot, another few inches and he would brake like the rifle. He pulled at the roll on his back, lifting it over his head, and throwing at the thing below, but this did little more than increase the downwards slide into the pit. He could make out the thick notches on the things skin, the tiny black wiry hairs of the creature working into the mud. His foot inches, less as his boot brushed against the huge worm and the thing frantically worked its direction to him. The mud to his burst revealing thinner strands of the tentacle, blunted and cone like as they reached up around him on both sides. The rain bouncing off the blunt tips, translucent with a blackened core.

A heavy blow struck Tommy's shoulder. The end inevitable and yet, he felt a tug upwards away from the dread below. His body jerked backwards as the blunted tentacles desperately crashed into his muddy imprint.

Then Carlson's face came into view, his whole body leaning into him, pulling him over the edge and away from the whirlpool of isolating flesh.

"Run, Son. Get out of here." Carlson hurled him in a

direction, his head tilted into the widening pit as they past it. "Don't stop for anything. You understand?" Carlson shouted, no longer the whisper, or the stooping in the shadows but a desperation to break free. "Run," Carlson said again as the ground broke ahead of them, wire and corpses towering above them and the monstrous object broke free of the dirt.

Its body thicker than a man with a series of lines around its sides as the rest of its mass disappeared into the ground. It pulsed forward, contracting and expanding rapidly towards them.

Carlson grabbed Tommy's shoulder again.

"Run, Son. It's all I've got to give." Carlson shoved him to the side, sending him backwards as the worm reared up. Carlson knife pressed outward from his chest. They met head on, the weapon sinking into the flat snout of the creature which resisted for a moment before bursting open. Tommy watched as Carlson sank forward into the creature, the skin of the beast falling around him, cocooning him in the sack of jellied flesh. Carlson kicked inside the creature, his arms beating at the side before he stopped, suspended as the thing reached to the sky and Carlson slipped further down, his movements slowing, before stopping completely.

Tommy grabbed at his waist, feeling for his mask, struggling against his damp hair until it scratched its way across his cheeks with the practice he'd honed. His own breath comforted him, warming against the numbness, filling the tiny glass windows with mist, which flickered back as he inhaled. The creature pulled back into the ground, Carlson's inert body flicking around with its movement as if it tried to sense more, to desire more. The mist filled the windows. Tommy shivered against the cold. His breathing settling until the mist on the inside of the visor subsided. Carlson no longer sat suspended in the creature's body. Both he and the thing had gone.

Tommy didn't run. He waited for the thing to emerge from the water logged hole and when he didn't, he still waited, still against the concave of a body he'd fallen into. The bones clawing at his rear and legs as the rain pelted against his mask.

The rain stopped as the morning sunrise appeared on the battlefield. First grey and then, colour of brown and green. Still, Tommy didn't move. His lungs stung, his eyes closed, and he fell back gasping.

White sheets covered him. He reached for his mask but couldn't find it.

"You wake," she said. Blonde hair the colour of sunflower brushed across him. "Don't move. They don't think live, but I knew." She stroked his arm. "War, not war. Over." She said. Each word carefully crafted in her accent. "You home? You wife?" She spoke, and he understood. "English not good yet. Oui?"

"Yes," Tommy said, his mouth cracking like dry earth.
The stone walls around him were solid and dry, built my man, and kept the rain away.

"You home now?" The girl asked. Birds chirped with early morning calls all around, overwhelming in their beauty. Tommy covered his ears. "Is loud, morning life calls, oui? You stay, home come, oui? We farm here."

Tommy rested his head back against the pillow. It swallowed him.

"I stay." He said. "Oui."

THE PHONE CALL

Her heart lept when it rang. It stayed out of place as she watched the phone vibrate on her desk, inching across the surface, it's light reflecting back against the polished wood and plastic casing. Of course it could be anyone, except she knew it would be her father.

She placed her pen on the paperwork she had been looking over and rubbed her hand across her mouth, eyeing the phone. She didn't know how she knew it would be him, she just did.

This would be her second conversation with him this evening, and one she could do without. Her eyes were heavy, it was late and too much work lay ahead of her to be distracted.

Picking up the pen, she lent forward over the spreadsheet and tried to follow each column. The insistent rumbles breaking through her concentration. What if it wasn't her father? Could there be a problem at the factory?

Ann sighed deeply and flipped the phone's case open. It indicated a withheld number. It had to be him.

It was difficult not to blame herself for the recent barrage of phone calls. When she first took over the business, much to the shock of her brother, she had delighted in their daily conversations. Her father, at last, had seen her worth. For the first time in her life, they had connected. In the past, it has always seemed that Tony had been favoured. He was older; the first born. They spent time together, playing sport and working on the business. Ann had wondered if it was because she was female, that they didn't get to spend so much time together when she was a child. He was always around of course, just his attention was drawn sometimes and she was left with her mother. In many ways, she took on his role as a carer, especially as time went by and her mother's illness got worse.

As time passed, and the business flourished under her watch, conversations on how things used to be run, were less important. She had the rights of things now. Tony could only look on from the sidelines of her victories. His money issues were no longer the business's problem and at last, a future for the company their father had crafted was possible. All down to her. Her phone calls had become less frequent, days passing into weeks between her calls. Until he started calling her.

She picked up the phone and slid her finger across the display to answer. Pressing the phone to her ear, she could hear the crackling of the line, always a feature of their telephone conversations.

"Hello. Ann?" Her father said on the other end of the

line. He always started in the same way, as though lost. Despite herself, the weight of the work she needed to finish, she smiled.

"Hi Dad. Of course it's me, who else would it be on this phone?" She said.

"I know sweetie, but it's difficult to know sometimes." She closed her eyes. The phone line hissed and crackled through the poor connection.

"So how are you sweetie? Is everything okay?" He paused, a small intake of breath. "I can't remember when we spoke last, it's strange because I think about our phone calls most of the time. They're so important to me."

"I know, Dad. I know." She looked at the computer screen's clock. It had been about two hours since they had spoke. The first, second and third ring she had ignored, tucking the phone under some papers. The forth she answered, in the hope it would be the last for the evening.

"What time is it there?" As though any time difference really mattered.

"Just gone midnight. It's late Dad."

"I see, and are you keeping well? How is Tony?"

"I'm good Dad. Just a little tired from working late. It's close to the end of the tax year so I need to get those accounts in order. You know how it is." She opened the desk drawer and looked at her to do list which seemed to be overfilled with jobs to complete. Her scrawling handwriting like an ink stained spider crawling across the page. She began to add to her list as a couple of other things came to mind.

Her father gave a low chuckle, more like a strangled choke. "Ann, you still there?"

"I'm here, Dad. Of course I am."

"Just checking. It's not always easy with the connection here. It's hard to tell if I'm speaking to you or not. You hear me Ann?"

"Yes, Dad." She tried to trace the figures across the columns with the pens nib.

"Years end. I know how that is. All those years working hard on things with your brother. It took its toll. Not just on me. If there is one thing I could change, looking back, it would be the amount of time I worked. It's different when you're in the midst of it. You think there is no other way, but the work will always wait. Trust me. Don't replace life with work or you're regret it."

Ann lost herself in his clarity. Lately, each call had seemed more or less the same, with each of them less connected to her reality. They had of course warned her of this, but she had been ready to shoulder the consequence of the situation. If truth be told, to have him ramble on about the same tired points of conversation gave a steady release, like air from a balloon slowly deflating. Eventually, it would be easy to let him go completely, but to hear him so lucid caught in the pit of her stomach like a clenched fist slow tightening.

"So what would you change Dad?" He remained silent. A faint buzz against her ear which grew louder, almost painful. Then, she was sure she heard it this time. A lowered voice in the background. Not her fathers, too low, too distant.

"I would spend more time with you all of course." He said, his voice breaking through the distortion in a monotone unlike him. He chuckled, pausing with that intake of breath again.

How she had longed to have him say this years ago, to act on it, and now, they seemed a pathetic collection of sounds.

"You can't take back the things you have done, no matter how much you want to. I know that now."

"What do you mean Dad? Is somebody there with you?" The fist clenched tighter pulling at her insides.

"I never got to thank you for looking after Mum all those years especially when she got really sick. I'll say it now. Thank you Ann."

She worked her mouth a little, struggling against the rising swell, her tired eyes aching with tears.

"I did what I had to Dad. We all did." She wanted to say she resented her mother for getting sick and dying before she had chance to become a mother herself. She wanted to confess she hated her mother for drinking so much that she had to help her to bed, even after she was in pain from her MS treatment. She wanted to say she blamed herself for her mother's death, because deep down she had wished for it to happen. Ann didn't say these things, nor did she say if he had been there for her mother, than maybe she wouldn't have to step in to the role.

"Is that you Ann?"

"Yes, Dad. I'm here."
"How is your brother, Tony? Is he there with you now?"
"No, Dad.' I'm on my own. They didn't speak anymore. Not since the legal battle over the business. Even before this they had found it difficult to tolerate each other. Just being in the same room made her mad. His bloated red face and bulging eyes made her wonder how they had been in anyway genetically

linked. He was incapable of any feeling, all he was ever interested in was the money. She didn't have the heart to tell him this, even though she wanted to draw him into saying something inflammatory about him.

"You are my daughter aren't you? Is it you Ann?" Again the low mumbling in the background as he spoke.

"I can hear somebody else. Dad, who's there?"

"Where, honey? Where am I?"

She couldn't do this again, not for the second time in as many hours, not with so much still to do.

"I must go. We'll speak tomorrow."

"I don't know when that is Ann. It's all the same. I get so lonely. There is only our phone calls, it's all I have." He raised his voice. "You understand me?" The vice like grip in her abdomen pushed a wave of nausea through her.

"I must go."

"I can't remember when I spoke to him last." Anger in his voice. "I want to speak to my Son!"

Ann could remember well when they had last spoke, when they had been together for the last time. It had been two years and fourteen days since her father had spoken to him. They had both gathered at the hospital to watch his gasping mouth and frail stick like arms battle with the air around him. She had watched her brothers emotionless face stand over her father as she held onto his scrawny hand. They said nothing as they listened to the monitors struggle further to keep his mechanisms going. Tony had whispered into his ear. Private words just for them, that she could never be a part of. Then he had died.

The doctors were called, they were asked to move back. The curtains were pulled, but that was the end.

"Dad, not now. I really must go. I'll get Tony over, get him to speak to you."

Her brother hadn't been around when she was approached by the After Life group. He had rushed away after an awkward embrace he had initiated with her. She could feel his body tense as it pressed against her own. The representative was already sitting in the corridor. She had only noticed the slim faux leather briefcase, with its cracked ends and his cheap suit after Tony had walked away. His thin hair combed across his head with great care; maybe once, he was proud of who he had dreamed of being. The business card had been pressed into her hand with a sense of urgency. Each objection had been smoothly countered leaving her in a position which she couldn't argue against. Of course she wanted to keep contact with her father. Of course she had things she still wanted to say. Of course she loved him.

"You lying…" The crackling on the line grew more pronounced. His voice became a fragmented electronic snap before quickly reverting back to his own. Ann pulled the thing away from her face. "I'm sorry, so sorry, sorry." His voice a tiny cry from the receiver. "Ann? Are you there? Ann?"

"I'm still listening."

"Its just that, lately I don't feel myself." He paused for that intake of breath, she knew was not necessary. It made her feel guilty She could hear the electronic rustle in the background and wondered how time passed for him. "Look don't worry about me Ann, I've called to find out all about you." He paused again. "I love you Ann. I don't know if I have ever said that." She smiled but her muscles felt strained and tired. He had said it of course, on a previous phone conversation but I guess it's different for him without a body. Maybe it's harder to keep things together, if there is no real container.

They had said there was a way to capture his... they had used the word essence. None of it made much sense really. It was all experimental, but if she gave permission, they could extract him before he was truly gone. They had to work now, so there was little time for much discussion. He would be taken and stored. Whenever she wanted to talk to him, he would be there. He had mentioned something about future possibilities. Enhanced video conversations were feasible in the future.

"Are you happy?" She asked.

There was no answer from her father. The lines static seemed more human now, like it was mimicking the way an electronic device would sound. She imagined him crying but knew this wasn't possible. After two years of calling, she found that she needed to less and less. Weeks would go past before she felt the need to call. That's when she began getting the calls from her father.

"I'm," he paused again. "Will you visit me Ann? Please will you come?" She knew where they were going now. When the conversation took on this trajectory, it was always difficult to listen to. Her father had never sounded desperate. He had never begged.

She had of course visited After Life. The offices listed were in a less than desirable part of the city. The doorway had smelt of urine. The sign over the buzzer was little more a plastic clip against masonry.

"Ann, I don't think I'm well. Please come." They had said all she needed to do was close the contract and they would disconnect. The phone would lose its service and the calls would stop. It was a simple process, but non reversible. She had asked what would happen to her father. The young lady working there had seemed confused by her question. Ann had left feeling embarrassed.

"I'll visit one day. Why don't you rest for now?" The phone felt hot against her ear.

"You promise Ann?" His voice lifting.

"I'll visit soon Dad. I promise. I must go for now. Love you."

"He says you're full of shit!"

Her body throbbed.
"Are you? Did you do this to me?" Again, the low rumbling voice in the background. "I'm disappointed if that's true. He says it's true."

"Who says it's true? Who is talking to you?"

"I'm forgetting Ann, but he tells me what to say. It hurts when I don't want the things to be true. I can't go on like this Ann, but he tells me there is a way. I can visit you. We can come to you tonight, now if he wants. Speak to him, Ann. Please speak to him." A crackle, her father tuning out, lost in a distance, muffled. "You wanted her." His voice far away.

Ann listened, shaking, heart pounding at the dragging of breath on the other end of the device.

She pulls the phone away, hanging up. The brilliant light of the screen fades back into the reflective darkness of the glass screen. So dark, it could be a void at the edge of space, untouched and unknown. Her own face looks back at her.

The screen lit up again.

Ann put the phone in the drawer. It's clattering vibrations louder than ever.

MEMORY OF A HEN PARTY

You press your back to the door. It's solid and reassuring. Tears sting the corner of your eyes and you snatch up some tissue and poke a triangle fold at the damp, not wanting it to ruin your makeup. Can't they see the effort you've put in! Not a single one of them offered to help and now all they can do was moan?

"Don't you think we should eat a little sooner? I need to eat before eight to keep the weight off?" *Well, you should have thought about that before I saw you stuffing that donut down at the train station, you fat bitch!*

"I hope you've checked they have gluten-free options?

And don't forget Rosie is vegan." *Well, you should have answered my e-mail that asked about meal options, Lilly, you lazy cow!*

"Really, a nightclub? I would have thought something a little classier. I'm sure you'll do better tomorrow, am I right?" *It's a hen-do Destiny! What do you want? Have any of you even met Amanda? She was pissed when she met Kevin, and if you ask me. To marry that lazy shit, she still must be. The least we could do is give her a good send off!*

"Have you arranged fizz for all the rooms? I don't want hubby thinking I'm out of control, especially as Tarquin's been teething and now he's all on his own to deal with him. I've promised a call every hour just to check, you know, give him a bit of support. You'll know all about all this if you have kids, if you ever meet the right person." *Well, don't drink it Felicity, you patronising...*

Look, none of them matter. It's all about giving Amanda a good time, showing her she has friends that care. She looked like she's having a good time, right?

You think about the whispering between Amanda and Lilly and your cheeks flush; you kick at your suitcase and throw your keys across the room. They crash against the lampshade, which falls to the floor with an uncomfortable smash. You imagine them all gathered in Lilly's room talking about you and how awful the whole long weekend will be. Well, if they will not enjoy it, you 're damn well not going to let it stop you from having a good time. The bottle is sitting chilled in an ice bucket exactly as you had arranged. Two glasses waiting impatiently. Well, more for me, you think, although you can't help the sense of wanting to sneak away; just grabbing your bag, heading down to the station with the bottle and enjoying a very relaxed train ride home.

"Oh, I thought it'll be best if I shared with Lilly. You know, with you being single and all. You never know you might get lucky." Amanda's eyes had flicked back to the rest of them standing behind her, a small smile twitching at the corner of her mouth and in that very instant, you were back at school. How you had hated school! The awkwardness of each day. Never being the right person, always the outsider.

Metal bands holding the cork fall away, letting the bottle burst open with a mockery of celebration. The beige liquid fills the glass, white bubbles fiercely pouring over the lip and down the smooth glass stem, spreading onto the table. The bubbles burst on your tongue and at the back of your throat as you take your first swig, which is chased by another. You guess you should get ready, but as you check your phone, you decide there is time enough.

You pour a second. Maybe you are overreacting. The entire weekend is ahead of you and Amanda could be right. What if you hooked up? Not that's your thing, but if you are ever going to meet the right person, you may need to step it up a gear. There is a playful knock at the door. You smile and take the glass with you, balancing it as best you can, some of the fizz coats your fingers. It's Amanda, no doubt, thanking you for all the effort that's gone into everything.

"Hey party girl," you say as you unlatch the door and pull it inwards. Only Amanda isn't there. It's the skinny man with the bad complexion from reception. He shifts uncomfortably as your smile sags.

"Hey,' he says. His gaze dropping to the ground. You both stand silently for a moment, him in the hushed corridor, the same beige as your drink. His neck takes on the colour of his uniform, shifting upwards along his neck and through his face until his cheeks burn crimson. You tap at the edge of the door, while the contents of your glass crackles, like static from a far away signal.

"Can I help?" You say finally. He almost flinches when you speak.

"I wanted to check I had all the details correct." You still say nothing. You assume he is talking about the chilled alcohol, chocolates and banners you'd asked to be placed in each room, but you keep staring. A part of you enjoys his discomfort. The momentary power which swells in your chest. "I took care of it as your requested on the phone. I just wanted to make sure everything was how you wanted. You were rather exact." Of course, he wants a tip.

* * *

You nod emphatically. "Of course, just a minute. Let me get my purse." You move back into your room.

"Really, there's no need," he says, but he's already crossed the threshold expectantly, holding the door open.

You rummage through your purse, flicking through the larger notes hoping to find something smaller. Coins spill out onto the crisp white sheets. You dismiss the idea of pushing change into his palm. A note comes free from the wad you had squeezed into it from the cashpoint. There is nothing smaller, and so resign yourself with a sigh to parting with it. After all, he had done what you asked.

"Do you have everything you need?" You don't respond, still reluctantly fingering the note with your back to him. "Is the bed comfortable enough?" His words scratch at the back of your mind and you suddenly feel anxious that this stranger is in your room.

When you turn, you notice he's looking about, his beady eyes taking in your overturned suitcase and keys now laying on the bedside table where the lamp should have been. Its wire sticks up from the socket and leads out to the unseen far side of the bed.

"Here," you say, quick to get back into his field of vision.

"No really, you don't have to." He takes it anyway and slips it into his back pocket in one smooth, well practiced flick. "It's only I noticed from our hallway CCTV that you're no longer sharing."

"Change of plan," you say sharply and begin to close the door on him. He doesn't move, however, his foot planted firmly against its base. Your breath catches, your scalp tingles, an invisible weight compresses against your spine. He looks up slowly. The eyes, a pale fragmented blue like the deep chill of frost. His cheeks are scarred and angry with his skin condition, you've done your best not to acknowledge. When he leans closer, you pull back, but the sourness of his breath still creeps inside you.

"I just wanted to check in. Make sure you 're not lonely." it's almost a whisper, as though he is sharing a secret. You can't swallow, can't think.

A door in the hallway opens and a giggling couple emerges. You glimpse the pair as she curls her head into the man's arm becoming a singular being which shambles towards the lifts.

"Thank you, I'll let you know if I need anything else," you say in a firm, loud voice. He pulls his foot from the doorway and you push it closed, resting your head against it, the flute of alcohol sloshing in your shaking hand. When you press your ear to the door, there is no sound on the other side. You'll warn the girls about the creepy hotel guy later, just to make them aware, add a little sparkle to the gossip.

"That's terrifying. You know what, maybe I should share with you after all." Amanda will say.

There is a ping on your phone, so you make your way over to read the message. It's Amanda.

I know you've booked us a restaurant, but Lilly has found another one for tonight, which has a wider menu. Hope you don't mind. X

Why should you care? Whatever keeps Amanda happy, it's her day. You squeeze the handset in your palm until the corners dig into your skin. The phone gives another muffled ping, sending a vibration through your arm. It's Lily this time.

Most of us are ready to go. I've booked a restaurant for a little earlier. Twenty Mins for taxi. Hurry.

With little thought, you down the alcohol, pour another and gulp at this as well. Then you pull out the contents of your suitcase, clothes spilling everywhere, until finally you find your deodorant and the makeup you'd carefully packed. Even after a few minutes, the shower still isn't warming up, so you skip this in favour of a cloud of artificial scents. You manage another glass. The bottle clangs noisily as you return it to the ice bucket and then pull it back out to swig the last of the dregs clinging to its bottom. Then you lean into the mirror, and work as quickly as you can, ignoring the furious pings on your phone.

You pause at the door, the lock half turned in your hand. You imagine him still there waiting. The door crashing open as he lunges at you, dragging you down onto the carpet. You inch the door open so that the hallway comes into view a fraction at a time.

There is nobody there.

Standing in the hall, you look into your bag one last time before letting the door go. The mechanism races to close before pausing just as it shuts, resting on a cushion of air created by its momentum. You wait for the satisfying click and give the handle a try, just to make sure it's locked before hurrying to the lifts. While you wait, you search the ceiling and the corners for the security cameras, but can't see anything obvious. Then again, they could hide them anywhere to not spoil the look of the place.

Finally, the lift arrives.

****

Despite holding the bag carefully, it still drops to the carpet. You gather yourself again, steadying yourself against the wall and lower yourself down. Only the floor slides to the side, taking your legs with it.

You find yourself on your arse. Lilly's voice rings in a pulsing blast of recollection.

"You're drunk and we've not even finished the meal. Don't spoil this for Amanda!"
Spoil! You arranged the whole God damn thing! You'd proved her wrong by walking down the centre of the restaurant, one foot placed in front of the other, balancing on an invisible tightrope, your arms raised, palms up, wine glasses sitting in each and not a drop spilt. Heads turned. Clearly somebody had to raise the tempo away from talk of flowers and seating arrangements. You could barely keep your eyes open through some of it. It wasn't your fault the waiter came out of nowhere.

Why make such a fuss about some broken glasses?

Carefully, with legs outstretched and your bag between them, you sort through the contents. You still can't find the keycard to let you in.This time you lay the things from your bag out onto the floor. There isn't much there, but still you can't find it. You'll just have to call one of the others. It doesn't matter if they've already gone to bed. Yet, you hesitate to open your phone case. When you do, the white rectangle of plastic falls out in front of you.

You 're on your knees holding out the key card to the tiny slot in the door, only the card is too thick, or the slot is too narrow. Even when you narrow your eyes with concentration, it doesn't slip in. When you've almost given up, finally it catches and the door lock clicks, allowing you to tumble forward into the dark interior.

On all fours, you make your way into the darkness of the hotel room, the door pressing into your side as you pull at your things lined neatly on the hallway carpet until you 're sure you have all of your possessions.

It's pitch black in your room with the door closed. You claw your way up the wallpaper in search of the light switch fingers swooshing back and forth. It's then you notice that something is wrong. It's in the darkness and everywhere around you. The sourness which leaked from the hotel porter lies heavily in the room, as though he is standing next to you in the dark.

You open and close your mouth. It's dry, sending a series of sticky clicks as you peer into the blackness. There you wait, your eyes struggling to make anything out at first, but as you stand frozen, you 're sure there is something watching from the corner. Your heart rattles. The floor beneath you creeks and you hold your breath.

Possibly a minute, maybe only a few seconds pass. It's hard to say, you 're frozen with fear and the weight of the darkness is crushing. A notification sounds from your phone. A dull thunk, you know well, indicates a low battery, and yet it spills light from its screen. You extend the screen at arm's length, turning the darkness into gloomy mounds.

A figure lies sprawled on the bed, the lump of body spilling impossibly long limbs across the mattress. An electric bolt ricochets across the front of your brain. You gasp, ready to turn, to pull at the door, to scream.

The light switch catches against your finger, and you flick the switch, showering the room with illumination. The only thing on the bed is the suitcase, your clothes stretched out from its partly open top, coiling onto the floor to finish in heaps at the foot of the bed. All your work. There is nobody in your room and yet, it's impossible to shake the idea of eyes watching you.

"Hello?" It's not your voice, but a weak, childlike cry. No reply comes. When you close your eyes, a fuzzy, dizzying sensation overtakes you. Cold water will help get your senses back and so you slide the door to the small bathroom, pulling the chord. An extractor whirs into motion as the light crackles against your reflection, but it's the warmth of trapped air in the room which makes your stomach lurch. Across the tops of the wall and the glass to the shower, beads of condensation trickle like perspiration. Your drunkenness propels you forward towards the sink, a desire to splash away the haze with cold, and yet the tap is hot against your touch. The beating of your heart drums against the silence as you look back out at your room.

You leave the bathroom in stages. At first a head, then a head and shoulders, until finally the whole of you emerges, plunging back into the scent. Skin crawling across your bones, as the smell swells and thickens the deeper into the room you go.
Every step you take is carefully placed as you make your way around and yet you still catch the desk painfully with your waist. The wine cracks against the metal sides of the wine

bucket. As you bend forward towards the drapping sheets of the bed, your balance shifts and you tumble face first to the ground, your temple crashing against the boxed underside of the bed. From your position on the carpet you can see the coils of dust, possibly a discarded tissue, but there is no room for anybody to hide. The room is empty, apart from yourself and the dead bits of fluff lingering from countless other guests. Certainly a comment to make in any reviews.

"You always have to pull everything down around you. Make a show. Construct a nightmare!" They were right, and in the sudden thickness of your drunkenness, it's clear to see. Then you notice the wardrobe is slightly ajar.

As you approach, you focus on listening for his exchange of breath behind the thin boards of the wardrobe door. There is a small gap at the centre, in which a flash of red is visible and your stomach twists as though its caught in a fall from a great height. Surely he sees you as well. There is only the flimsiest of barriers between you. At any moment, he could spring forward, overpowering you as you collapse back on the bed. The instant you turn to run, his hands will spring out and tighten around your neck.

Looking around, all you can see is the bottle still poking from the silver bucket. Once in your hand, water runs against your knuckles and along your arm as you raise it in readiness. The temptation to run overwhelms you, and yet you can't move, can't turn your back on the slither of uniform you see through the gap. Your dieing phone in one hand, the neck of the empty bottle in the other.

It all happens at once.

You see movement as you peer into the gap. There is no choice but to lunge at him, your whole body crashing against the door, the bottle clatters against its side, catapulting from your grip. A cracking of wood, sudden and alarming from against your back as you feel yourself being dragged inside, the lifeless reflective surface of your phone in your hand as you struggle to stay upright. Then there is the embrace.

Flailing arms and legs do nothing to stop the attack as red cloth covers your face, and a coat hanger entangles your arm, a blow to your back all but knocks the cry from your lips and you wheeze at the tangle of fabric. His touch is light against your body, his weightlessness pressing down on you.

Forcing yourself forward, you roll away from the attacker with ease. The red dress you'd bought especially for the weekend, the only thing you'd taken pride with before you dashed off for the evening, half hangs on a twisted wire hanger. It sits lopsided, flapping with a rip to its side, like a body sliced open. One of the wardrobe doors hangs closely from its hinges. The other you've snapped across its centre. Apart from this, the wardrobe is empty.

It's all a mess. Not just your the dress, the weekend, you.

Crawling across the room, you reach up and scramble on to the bed. It's so much higher than the one you have at home. It's uncomfortable, lumpy and jagged, but you are beyond caring. The room swirls around, until you blink at the ceiling and there is a moment of steadiness before it all starts again. You flop the phone next to you, the same companion who shares your bed night after night, and close your eyes. They hurt. Light flickers like thousands of tiny shards of glass reflecting moonlight in the back of your head. You struggle to keep your breath steady, as it multiples and envelops you before you sleep. Once again the sourness surrounds you, and with a bitter laugh you realise it was you all along.

*****

The first thing you notice is the pounding at the front

of your head and the coarseness of your throat. Light struggles around the corner of the curtains and rain patters heavily on the glass.

When you raise yourself in the unfamiliar surroundings. The carnage shocks you before you catch up with the empty glasses and overturned bottle, clothes thrown across the floor, the broken wardrobe door and finally the missing lamp. You know full well the fragments lay shattered on the floor. Next came the recollections of the night before, uncomfortable and jarring as the fragmented images burst like unwanted guests into your thoughts.

The phone vibrates next to you. There is an uncomfortable disconnection with this. A stifling anxiety which makes you want to roll over and never exist and yet you pick it up and look at the screen.

The time shows at gone four in the afternoon. How could you have possibly slept for so long? You've never been so hung over, or so drunk, if it comes to that! There are several messages on the screen face. The first from Lily.

What's wrong with you. Why would you go out of your way to spoil everything?

Then another similar from Rosie. You press the one from Amanda which reads: *If that's the way you're going to be. Consider us done!*

Perspiration engulfs you as your whole body catches fire at the message you had sent her in the early hours of the morning. Each word an empty wine bottle pounding against your head.

Think damn it!

The room was in darkness. You remember the search, holding out your phone before the battery died, and yet you there it is, fully charged, your message to Amanda clear for you to see.

We're done as friends. I'm tired of not being appreciated. I'll be on the first train out of here. Don't contact me when you get back. Or ever.

Your insides curl and twist over on themselves as though a snake has entered you in the night. You recall the search, your positivity of being watched, and that odour which still lingers. It's on your skin and the folds of the sheets as you stretch your hand away from you across the surface of the empty bed space next to you, feeling the lumps and bumps of the mattress.

It sighs as if from the pleasure of your touch.

The shock jerks you upright.

A ghostly exhale of air sends another overpowering wave of bitterness into the room, your eyes wide in their sockets, as you stare at the white cotton. Carefully you ease the folds back, sliding the sheet across the bed, the stained, yellow mattress revealed little by little. First the raised edges of fabric around its corners, stitched tightly to bind the filling. Next you see the decorative swirls of pattern, but there is no mistaking it. As the sheet recedes, a viscous tear, the filling spilling out slightly against the loose cloth.

An explosion of fear bursts painfully against your ribs. A crack of madness whirs inside your lungs, forcing a low moan, like a sensless creature led to slaughter.

Fingers wriggle up through the tear, struggling against the taught fastening momentarily until it gives and an arm bursts free and then another and you understand the outline carved into the thick layers of foam. A face forms against the material, its mouth gasping as if trying to taste the surrounding air, a pale blue eye fixing you as you fall backwards, toppling, your scream knocked away. He is quick. The emergence just for show. His pale damp skin writhing against your body, a cloth, bitter and dizzying, traps the emerging scream.

The last thing you recall is the couple from the hallway, collapsing into each other as if they were one.

GRAND BREAKFAST

Mr Otto shifted uncomfortably in his his seat. A problem in many dining facilities he had encountered time and time again over the years, but he expected better at this establishment, especially for the price.

"Let me show you how to deal with this," he said. "Watch and learn, Jamie. You'll be old enough to come and work in the family business soon and if there is one thing about life, a man who makes money controls his dining experience."

Mr Otto attempted to shift back from the table, but his vast belly and consequently weight made it difficult for him to lift his seat, the white linen cloth clamped tightly between the balloon of his stomach and the underside of the table. The salt and pepper bottles rattling together in the centre as he twisted.

"Does it matter dear? It's only breakfast, we're on holiday." His wife said, reaching over to settle the two shaking canisters.

"Of course it matters! This is the way we begin our day. What kind of person would endure discomfort and dissatisfaction with any meal, let alone the one which fuels the stove and powers you on to success?" Otto turned to his son. "Listen, my boy. Never accept what you are given at face value. Always demand more, as excellence is around the next corner."

Jamie, at seventeen, wasn't as large as his father yet, although he had made a magnificent effort to be his father's son regarding his size. Jamie still suspected his father's dissatisfaction with him. The speeches kept getting longer, trickling through his mind like custard.

"Do you hear me Jamie?" Otto pushed the mass of his neck back to stare at his son. Jamie's mouth hung open, his eyes two dull lights barely twinkling under the grand windows of the breakfast room. His hands, two large hunks of fat, fingers bloated as they drummed with impatience.

"We've been waiting ages now. I'm starving! We only ordered a cooked breakfast, I could have made it myself by now." Jamie said.

"I'm sure it's coming. Lets not make a fuss about everything we do. Instead, why don't you think about the day ahead. Make some plans for the holiday. I thought we could start with a pleasant walk along the promenade and take in the sea air."

Mr Otto sighed. "We are not making a fuss Sandra, we are merely ensuring we get what we deserve. That's how I have always conducted myself, that's how I've always done the best for this family. Would we have our house without me pushing for the best? I think not. Would they have awarded me Slough's small business man of the year…"

"Business person." She corrected.

"Very well." Mr Otto wobbled with impatience. Slough's small business *person* of the year? It's all the same, Sandra. The point is, everything you enjoy is down to me and the way I conduct myself. Are you listening Jamie?'

Jamie wasn't listening. His stomach growled with impatience. Everybody else in the room seemed to be tucking into piles of food while they sat with empty plates. His mouth watered every time the door to the kitchen swung open. Then, just as his father had begun another part of the same speech he always gave, Jamie saw the tray being pushed through the doors.

"My boy, you must have a hunger if you want to be successful. You must always seek…"

"Here it comes, Dad." Mr Otto's face crumpled with impatience at being interrupted. He looked across the room, stroking down the front of his shirt as he did so.

A man in an ill-fitted jacket and trousers, all bones, meandered through the dining space. He pushed a silver trolly, it's two shelves full with assorted breakfast boxes along with two domed food covers. The man's face was gaunt, his complexion the colour of ash, his cheeks drawn, which gave the appearance of an elongated deformity, his jawline stretched. He paused at another table, smiling widely at a family of four. His teeth were in contrast to his unhealthy complexion, gleaming impossibly as he leaned into the family, answering a question Otto couldn't make out, and then began a conversation. The server's turning his back on Otto on his family as he made gestures, the family enraptured by his conversation.

"Would you look at this? This is exactly what I mean? You give these people your custom, and this is the kind of service you get."

"He's only being polite." Sandra said.

"While our breakfast gets cold! This is what I'm talking about!"

"Your breakfast is getting cold, I ordered the cereal remember?"

"That's not the point Sandra! It's the customer bloody service!" Mr Otto raised his voice significantly so that the tables closest drifted out of their own conversations and give them curious glances.

"Mind yourself, remember what the Doctor said about your cholesterol levels. We don't need you all worked up."
"I don't care what the Doctor said about any of that nonsense. My father ate whatever he felt and he lived of a ripe old age."
"Didn't he die of a heart attack?"

"Caused by stress dealing with unions and such forth. He was a fine figure of a man all other respects. Now hush, here he comes."

Sandra closed her eyes, as was her way of dealing with her husband. She often wished to have her lids tightly shut through most of their time together. Instead, she busied herself, not purposefully at first, but as the years evaporated around her, and Jamie grew, she found her timetable filling up. The gym, her tennis club and art classes occupied her, but the list of clubs seemed to be ever expanding like her husband's waistline.

The man brought the trolly to a halt next to their table. Two silver domes covered plates, while a selection of small boxes and fruit sat next to them. Mr Otto looked at Sandra's fruit and cereal dismissively.

"Good morning," the server said, using the same broad smile he had used on the previous guests "I trust you slept well. You have the best rooms in the hotel. Wonderful rooms those with a superb view of the coast. You know, at its best, this hotel had all the celebrities, and they all demanded that room. Those were the days."

Mr Otto looked down at the breakfast trolly. Jamie also seemed enraptured by the trolly. The thick slab of his tongue licking his lips. The server looked at each of them before realisation made him jerk to attention, his back straightening, his hands poised over the silver domes.

"What am I thinking? You must be famished after such a luxurious night of rest. Please allow me." He placed the plates on the table in front of Otto and his son and quickly arranged the cereal for Sandra. "Enjoy." He pulled the lids away, unveiling the breakfast with a flourish.

Mr Otto pulled back over his chins at the sight of them. The shrivelled pair of sausages, the thin strip of bacon, the smear of beans and the teaspoon of egg which greeted him. Jamie grabbed at his fork, jabbing at a sausage and thrusting it towards his mouth. Otto knocked it away before Jamie could squeeze it past his cheeks and into the cavernous abyss.

"This is not enough!" His face grew red and then purple. An old lady two tables over gave them a bewildered glance, adjusting her glasses on the end of her nose.

"Now, dear. Remember the Doctor." Sandra rested her hand on the back of her husbands, her touch reminding him of something between them, like the last flicker of a candle flame. He pulled his hand away to point at the server.

"To hell with the Doctor. This is not a full breakfast! It's merely a suggestion of a breakfast. I have taken my family to some of the best restaurants in the country. We have eaten some of the rarest ingredients cooked by top chefs and this isn't good enough to give to my dog!"

"Dad, we don't have a dog."

"That is not the point, Jamie. The predicament I'm trying to clarify for this person is that the food he has placed in front of us is substandard, especially for the price we have paid to stay here."

"Is it not what you ordered, Sir?" The man reached for a small box of cereal and opened it, his knuckles showing white through the skin on his hands. "Madame, did you not ask for a light breakfast?"

"This man!' Otto said, lifting the plate and letting it fall back to the table with a clatter. One sausage rolled to the edge. They all watched it as it plopped onto the white of the tablecloth, leaving a brown stain. "This stale offering is not good enough, not for me and certainly not for my growing boy."

The server looked at Jamie, who was staring longingly at spilled sausage.

"I see." He produced another fork. Seemingly from thin air and held it out to Jamie. Otto grabbed at it, knocking it onto the floor with the tips of his heavy fingers. He hadn't noticed the stillness in the room, the hum of conversation fading, so that all attention focused on them. Sandra could sense nothing else, like she was the centre of a stage show. She pushed her bowl away from her.

"Sir, I assure you, we use the finest produce and have a prime chef to prepare every meal to the exacting standards of every one of our customers. If you are unhappy, we will certainly do everything we can to ensure your dining experience is a pleasure."

"It's a little too late for that, don't you think?" Otto shouted. I have a good mind to speak to your manager about the poor service and the poor quality. Even the seats are inadequate!"

"The seats? Nobody's complained about the seats before."

"Yes the seats, man! How is anybody supposed to have comfort in these tiny things? Don't you agree Jamie? Well, speak up!"

Jamie spluttered. A thin orange line dribbled from his mouth and he tried his best to both chew and speak with a mouth full of beans he had scooped in using his knife.

"Well," Jamie struggled. "It's not what my father expects. We have high standards and well..." He trailed off as bean fell onto his belly.

"Get me the person, in charge."

The thin man straightened.

"I'm in charge."

"Not you! I want the organ grinder and not the monkey. The manager or owner or somebody who has some authority here, man. It's not good enough, I tell you."

"I'm the manager and owner of the hotel. I assure you sir, if there is anything I can do to readdress things…"

Mr Otto threw his head back and looked up to the ornate plaster mouldings. "Well that explains a lot! You can start by getting me a decent breakfast and assuring me that every aspect of the rest of my stay will be up to my precise specifications."

"I understand, sir. I can only apologise for my negligence, sir. Please allow me to take this away and get you another."

"And how long will we have to wait? I think it is best you leave this for now, and I'll expect a real breakfast, exactly as I like it forthwith."

"Forthwith, sir. Of course, sir. I understand." The manager turned and pushed the tray away, the metal clanging as it bumped across the carpet, heads following him as he went. The silence slowly replaced by hushed murmurs and cutlery on plates.

Otto jerked on his seat in an effort to readjust himself to face Jamie, the chair groaning under his bulk.

"Did you have to make such a scene, dear?"

"You can't set low expectations. Isn't that right Jamie?" Jamie held one of the sausages in his palm, his mouth open ready to absorb it.

"I'm going to my room, I've totally lost my appetite." Sandra said.

"That's the difference between us. I have a never ending appetite. That's how you make things happen."

Sandra got up from the table. She ignored the twisting necks, focusing on her as she passed by. Instead, she focused on the grandness of the hotel caught in the tiny details, the polished oak panelling, the swirls of colour on the carpet, the decorative faces on the door handle to the dining hall, until she had left them behind.

"He's coming back," Jamie said through a mouthful of food.

Once again he appeared with the rickety trolly and placed the food on the table, revealing a large plate full to brimming with a full range of sausages, crispy slices of bacon, still glistening with fat, hard-boiled eggs lined up on little silver stands, slices of black pudding all set to topple off the plate.

"This is more like it what we requested, at last."

"I must say, I am sorry we did not meet your expectations. The chef especially is deeply embarrassed. As a way to make amends for a lack of focus, we would very much like to invite you to our special dining experience. We usually reserve this as an event for a most exacting of customers. I promise it to be one of the most delectable treats you will ever experience and will set the standards for any other meal in the future. I do hope you will let me make this gesture."

Otto pulled himself upright. "As I would expect."

"You can, of course, bring your family. There will be no

cost, as a gesture of our good intentions, including any beverages you wish to have." He placed a small black card with silver lettering on the table. "It's in our private members' rooms at eight this evening. You are more than welcome to inspect the food in their preparation, but I trust you we will not disappoint."

"We will see about that," Otto said shortly before reaching over with his fork to stab violently at an enormous slab of black pudding, followed by a huge scoop of egg. The manager hovered, his smile faltering as he watched Otto chew, glistening fat oozing at the sides of his mouth. He paused, the manager nodded and backed away, pulling the trolly behind him as he left.

* * *

Jamie and Otto squeezed into a lift when it finally arrived. The old woman from the dining suite stood behind them and struggled to see room for herself. Otto closed the door with a push of a button without giving her a second thought.

"Do you see my boy? That's how we get things done in our family. Once you set standards, others need to meet it. It's that simple. A good appetite for life makes things happen, and that applies to business just as much." He rested his hand on his belly and belched, filling the metal coffin with the smell of partly digesting meat.

Jamie turned over the card the manager had presented to them. "It's a black-tie event it says."

"I should think so. I imagine the rest of the common folk aren't invited to such things. I'll show you the right ways to mingle and strike up a deal. That the way of things, it's all about who you know."

* * *

"What do you mean your not coming? It's a black tie event." Otto lay on the bed in his stretched underwear.

"I don't like these kinds of things. Not really. While I was out today, I saw a show I wanted to attend. That's why we're here, to do the things we don't get to do at home, not lounge around the same hotel all day."

"Well, I was full after breakfast wasn't I, and needed a lie down."

"I've laid out your suits for both Jamie and yourself, but I'd much rather go to the show. I'm sure Jamie would too."

"He has to learn, Sandra. You have never been involved in business and this is how it's done."

"Well, enjoy yourself, and don't have too much wine. You know how you get."

"Your leaving now? Why don't you come and lie next to me?" Otto patted the crinkled bed sheets which inclined steeply under his bulk. "As you say, it's a chance to do the things we don't have time for at home."

Sandra stiffened, her mouth pressed into a tight smile.

"Oh." She looked around the room and towards his clothes hanging from the wardrobe door. "Time! We'll have more time tomorrow. You don't want to be late and I've already got myself mentally prepared for the show. It's the one my friend recommended to me."

"Not the same friend who gave you the details on this place? Well I hope you tell her I'm not impressed with the suggestion, and if the hotel is anything to go by then your show is sure to be a disaster." He sighed and pulled himself over to his side with one hand reaching into his underwear to give himself a good scratch.

She closed the hotel room door behind her and stood in the corridor. She could hear her husband heaving himself off the bed. The mattress springs clanging beneath him. She took a step towards Jamie's room, after all she had played some roll in raising him after his mother had left. All those tantrum's she had endured, the torture of pretending she cared for him. At any rate, it was easier than the fantasy between her and that fat cash pile. Finally she could be free of them both. Sandra smiled and made her way towards the lifts with a dance in her steps.

***

They made their way down to the reception. Jamie continually adjusting his shirt collar where his neck spilled over. Otto attempting to squeeze the buttons of his jacket together. Both of them to lost in their own discomfort to take in any of period features of the lobby, the rich mahogany bookshelf lined with leather bound tomes. They especially didn't notice the hungry eyes on them as they shuffled over to the reception desk.

The manager, who had been gently chatting to another patron, uncurled himself and slipped towards them on his spindly legs. Despite being at the other end of the lobby, he was easily able to intercept them before they got any where near to the receptionist. That same smile creeping from ear to ear, showing off the deformity of his ill proportioned facial features once again.

"I'm so glad you 're on time and so splendidly dressed." Jamie looked down at himself, only just able to see the tips of his shoes, his cheeks burned crimson. Otto looked up to the manager. Now that they were all standing, he realised how tall he was in comparison to himself and Jamie, and almost anybody he had ever met. "Please allow me to show you to the members' suite for the last meal you'll ever want. That I promise."

Jamie's eyes blazed before settling back into the deep pits of his face. His tongue slipping out over his lips.

"I hope you have an appetite young man," he said to Jamie, placing arm, rather informally Otto thought, around his son's shoulders.

The manager led them to a door, Otto arched his brushy eyebrows at the large gold italic lettering over the frame although struggled to read the script, not that he would admit this. Curiously, he hadn't given it a second glance at any other time, even though now they stood ready to enter it was hard to ignore.

"You would not believe how steeped in history this exclusive club is. Over the many years, we've had many very special members, some of them very prominent in society. I can't give names, you understand, but many of them are in the public eye daily and have a great interest in how the country runs. I say to much. Forgive me."

"I understand. I, myself am involved in many influential groups. It has its advantages, if you cross the right palms with silver, so to speak." Otto chuckled. The manager looked at him flatly before pushing the door open.

He was unsure what he expected. Possibly, a board room filled with dignitaries, or a vast hall swirling in notables. Again, it seemed the disappointment of the breakfast was repeating on him.

The only light came from several flickering candles. Thick drapes hung across the windows giving a sense of containment and secrecy to the space. A small room, not much larger than his own living room back home, housed the faded greens and browns of several dusty armchairs, in which sat three of four equally dusty occupants. None of them seemed to have much time left. Grey skin and hair twisted into shrivelled suits. Most seemed oblivious to their guests entrance, preoccupied in scrutinising folded newspapers, or reaching a shaking hand for a small glass, which continually seemed out of reach. One of them could have been asleep, or if not asleep, Otto could only have concluded he'd died. A younger man, still with the side flecks of grey in his hair, ran his fingers across a bookshelf in the far corner. He glanced back at them with a distant look and returned his attention to rows of spines without the slightest interest of the visitors. Nearest the door they had entered through, a piano was set against the wall. A woman, in a dappled cream dress, which may have once been pure white, tried her best to focus on the sheet music in front of her. Her hand hovered over the keys. Then she returned them to her lap, with a frown at Otto, as though he had interrupted her concentration.

The manager gently closed the door behind them and with hands on backs ushered them forward across the carpet before Otto could muster his protest.

"I though you said this would be a grand occasion, Dad?" Jamie whispered. Otto pulled himself upright, turned on the manager just as a slender woman drifted from out of a shadowy corner.

"Is this them? Well, I must say it is very exciting to meet you. We have been positively starved of a decent company as of late. It's about time, Hubert, we had some fresh additions to proceedings. Don't you think?" She swirled her coils of blond hair, so perfectly styled it oozed expense. "Fresh blood." She leaned into Otto. "I can't tell you how often I've said this, and how many times Hubert has ignored me."

"Not now, Angelic. They'll be time enough for you to enjoy with our guests, but please let them settle in first."

"Come now Hubert. How can we lead a country without a little life in the organisation. I trust you have seen something special here."

Angelic placed her hand out for Otto, who straightened up formally, taking it in his plump fists and raising it to his mouth where he gave it a gentle kiss.

'Enchanting.' Otto said. Jamie snorted causing Otto to glare at him.

Angelic ran her fingers against her dress before spinning, the dress twirling around her in a flutter of crimson as she glided around them.

"Oh, I love him Hubert. I could eat him up. He's adorable."

Otto bristled at the attention and the shifting stares of some of the seated gentlemen.

"Please, Angelic. This is not the time. Their dining experience is ready and chief will be rather cross if it's to spoil. Don't you think?"

Angelic pouted, giving her a fleeting look of a mischievous girl wanting to get her own way, before smiled thinly, her pearl white teeth gleaming against the candles burn.

"What am I thinking? Please enjoy."

The manager, Hubert, led them across the room and opened another doorway to a corridor lined with rich burgundy curtains. Jamie brushed his hand against them, the tips of his fingers catching the coldness of the walls beneath.

"I will say, this is not as I was expecting. I'm unsure this is the right fit for somebody of my high position."

Hubert raised an eyebrow.

"If only you could understand the influence in that one room. Those represent some of oldest members, not all our guests have arrived. As you can imagine, powerful people have busy agendas, and the night is still young. Now allow me to get you seated."

The corridor was narrow for them to walk in anything other than single file. Hubert took the lead, while Jamie and Otto, nudged against one another, until Jamie squeezed in behind the Manager.

"Everything in this part of the hotel dates back and is of the finest, as I hope you'll see. We have a wine list of course, but may I recommend the wine dating back to 1898, lovely year and very expensive, not that it matters while you are with us."

"Is membership expensive?" Jamie asked. Otto gave him a warning kick catching Jamie's heel.

"We, as a rule, don't discuss costs, but I may say that monetary values are not of significance for our members. There is more a lifetime agreement, shall we say?"

"I may need to discuss this further after we have dined.' Otto said, puffing out his cheeks. "I believe there is a great deal we could offer such an organisation."

"May I say, sir. You would not be here, if we didn't think you had a lot to offer our club. Here we are."

The manager opened a padded door which sat in the middle of the corridor. The curtains continued past it. I've taken the liberty of giving the red some time to breathe.

The space in front of them was much larger than the last room, the table laid beautifully with all manor of trappings associated with luxury. The same red tapestry surrounded the room while a large candelabra rested in the middle of the table.

"Where is everybody else?" The same flicker of doubt, he had when first walking into the members club twisted in his gut.

"I apologise, If I didn't make this clear. The dining experience is intimate, food for you to enjoy. There will be opportunity to see our members once you have eaten your fill, so to speak."

Hubert, made his way to the wine bottle resting on the table and poured a little in each of the two glasses.

"None for the boy. He's not of age just yet."

"As you wish sir, but it would be a shame for him not to a least sample such a unique wine."

"Please Dad. Just a little."

"Very well, my boy. Just a little mind."

"I can assure you, sir. There is plenty to go around." Hubert nodded at them both and left, closing the door gently behind him.

"Dad, I think this is gold." Jamie said picking up one of the napkin rings. Otto examined his own, eyes widening.

"I believe you're right. Where there is power, there's money. They go hand in hand, in the world."

Otto settled into one the chairs more akin to thrones than spindly mesh of seating he'd gotten used to for so long. The padding comforting his ample frame with ease.

"This is more like it, I must say. Take a seat, Jamie. Don't stand around dumbfounded. Like I say, if you have an apetite for success, you get what you deserve."

"Don't you think it's all a bit odd, Dad to have a secret room, like this. A hidden organisation hiding in a hotel, it's all a bit… weird."

The boy still had so much to learn. Otto rolled his eyes and sipped at his wine glass. It fell against his throat, thick and strong. Jamie picked up his glass and sampled the contents gingerly at first before slurping back the contents. The red staining his teeth and lips.

"Do you think they'd notice if one of these went missing?' Jamie said holding up a gold napkin ring and giggling.

"Don't embarrass yourself, Jamie." Otto said, although the thought of them sitting impressively on his own dining table back in Slough had already crossed his mind. "And not too much more wine for you, it's a strong vintage." Even as he said this, his words felt stretched and incomplete, the room taking on a warm glow of comfort.

The door opened and Hubert walked in once more.

"Ah, this is a lovely wine, my good man and such a splendid room. I must say how much of a surprise it is to have this buried in the heart of such a hotel.
"Please allow me, sir." Hubert poured another, larger volume into each glass. The liquid trickled gently, folding in on itself in and endless cascade, the light catching across the sur-

face.

"I'll be in shortly with the first course. Please take the time to enjoy the flavour of this very special year. I remember it so well." The manager bowed and closed the door quietly once again behind him.

"Remembers?" Jamie snorted. He took large swig from the heady liquid. Otto couldn't think what he was talking about and stared at him blankly. Jamie turned his head to the side as though he was trying to decipher a code. "That's what he said, remember?"

Otto spoke slowly "Control yourself, boy. That's your last glass. You hear me?"

"Whatever you say, Dad."

The door opened once again. The manager took two small plates topped with the familiar domes, only these were ornate with beautiful carvings.

"I trust you found the wine agreeable, gentlemen. It is one of our finest.' He placed the plates delicately onto the table in front of them both. 'Allow me."

He pulled off the cover. Both Otto and Jamie leaned forward eagerly.

"Is this some kind of joke?" Otto said casting a glance back to Jamie's plate and then his own.

"No joke sir." Hubert span and left the room. "Please don't rush. Savour every mouthful."

"What is this? I've a good mind to go out there and teach that jumped up…" Otto rocked on his chair.

"It looks amazing. I don't think I've ever seen anything so tasty and the smell."

"What are you talking about. The plates are empty, Jamie. They are trying to prove a point. Make a fool of me. Ridicule me in front of these so called important members. Well I won't have it I tell you!"

Jamie pulled the plate towards him, his tongue hanging limply out of his mouth. I don't think I've ever seen anything so delicious. Jamie snatched up one of the steak knives which had already been laid out.

"Jamie, what are you talking about. I will not stand for this." He banged his hand on the table but rested it on a one of the knives as well.

Jamie pulled his plate closer placing his huge sausage fingers against the china. He wriggling them against the white and held the knife over the index finger just below the nail.

"So fresh and succulent."

"What are you doing Jamie?" But as he said this, an insatiable hunger grabbed at him, gnawing at his insides.

Jamie pressed the knife against his finger, sawing back and forth at the skin.

"It cuts like butter, it's so well cooked." The blood didn't flow at first, allowing him to get quickly to the bone before his plate filled with the rich thick red of his son's life blood. The sharpness of the metal clacked as he scraped the meat off against the bone. Jamie opened his mouth taking the tip of a finger and placing it on his tongue, chewing slowly as to savour the flavour. "Oh it's wonderful, you must try some."

Otto couldn't speak, he held his tongue with his fingers as he brought the knife against the flabby pink flesh. His eyes widened as he noticed the red curtains pulling back as though on some automated track. A crowd of people stood eagerly leaning against the revealed glass underneath. Angelic stood at the forefront, her hands clenched, her wrists wires.

Otto grunted. He could say little more. His knife sliced back and forth until the wriggling piece of meat fell onto his plate. Blood spilled over his chin, and down onto the white of the shirt. The group clawed at the glass with exploding delight.

He felt no pain, only the delicious texture and full flavour as he swallowed a mouthful of the most succulent food he had ever tasted, knowing he would eat nothing like it ever again.

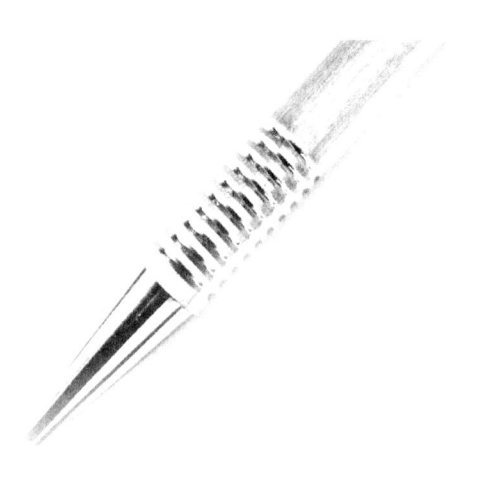

CLONES

I fold the trousers into squares, and take equal care with the shirts, placing each of them a meter in front of the capsules' exits. Next, I lay the small vials of liquid in the centre. They nestle in the soft, white fabric like a prize being presented in a ceremony. I make sure that each glass bottle sits identically. The red light blinks through my preparations, a visual heartbeat out of rhythm from my racing pulse.

The frosted glass panels of the cloning pods are difficult to see through, revealing nothing more than a dark motionless outline inside the chamber. My stomach tightens, sending ripples through my core. I move back to the notes on the table, turning the pages thoughtfully, only able to read when the crimson flair has flicked to white. The notebook is at odds and needs to be adjusted so that it sits squarely with the other assorted apparatus. I move the tubes and heavy stands around, until I'm satisfied, resting the pen in the pad's groove, then picking it up again to underline a key passage. A sudden hissing makes me turn as clouds of steam emerge from under the rising glass of one of the cloning booths.

I clear my throat. 'So, what am I working with?' I say, while smoothing out my shirt. Despite my calm stance, my chest thumps powerfully, drumming, so that it's hard to hear my voice. A wave of heat sweeps through the room as the steam dissipates. It's once ample proportions squeeze against me. I know full well what is at stake. I wait to see him emerge.

The panelling ascends over the upright casket, pushing the last of the hot air out into the room. Perspiration nestles thickly against my brow, trickling against the side of my cheek. There is no movement. No convulsion as consciousness takes hold of the clone. My mouth is as dry as ash. The open cloning station burns red with the light. I hold back, coughing to loosen the thickness gripping my insides, not daring to peer inside.

The process, of course, can be unpredictable. Recreating a perfect duplicate to the original, despite the term clone, is difficult. There are many variables with the human form and especially the brain, which makes the species difficult to replicate and prone to many neurological disorders.

Through the doorway to the booth, I snatch a glimpse of pale flesh, a jerking movement which indicates some form of life lurking inside. I take another step forward, legs trembling, the floor meeting each footfall too quickly, and yet through sheer will, I keep my balance. Closer, its breathing is deep and resonating. One long inhalation followed by a deep exhalation of a wakening beast.

I reach the front of his pod. His body lies at a gentle angle. A sheen of sweat covers him, his hair damp and darker than my own because of it. Nevertheless, the replication is uncanny. My skin crawls at the sensation of seeing a copy of myself. It's my brown eyes swivelling around in the sockets. I can't help the nausea, but I don't let it show. His head seems well proportioned, his shoulders narrow and breast tissue forms into two lumps, which I must admit makes me a little ashamed, if this is indeed how my own body may appear from an outside observer. His midsection is larger than the width of the shoulders with notable bilateral overhangs of fat just above his… I stop when I get to the unnecessary erection, which twists my insides.

'Clothes!' I say, pointing at the neat pile I'd taken care to assemble. He shambles forward, his mouth falling open in idiotic fashion before grabbing at his phallus with a hand and steading himself on the edge of the pod with another. 'Can you hear me? Put on the clothes.' His tongue lolls out over the corner of his lips as he moves the hand, clutching his member in rapid bursts. The resemblance I'd noted on first examination falls away, as he shifts his gaze around the room without focusing on anything in particular. He creases his brow. But I doubt it can process much. The inner functionality of the mind is just as important as the physicality, acting in unison to create a satisfactory replication. I still hold the pen and click it formally, as if preparing to record my observations.

'You need to drink from the glass vial. Your body won't cope now you're out of the chamber. It provides your body with a quick influx of the enzymes to kick start an immune response and a regulatory system away from the mechanics of the cloning station…' He grabs at his penis with both hands, drool dripping down his chin as he lets out a low moan of vowels, reminiscent of an early species of human. 'Do you understand?' I already know he doesn't. He gives me a blank, unintelligent stare before jerking his erection again in response.

I reach down to the clothes and thrust them up at him, knocking the vial. It clatters across the room and comes to rest at the wall. He darts for it, lumbering, half bent, using a combination of his one free arm and legs to propel himself. Its other hand still rakes at genitalia.

'Just put on some clothes, will you?' I throw the bundle of fabric at him. He dodges it and backs into a corner, making that frantic animalistic sound.

He will not survive long without the balance of chemicals. Already, his movements have slowed, those familiar eyes developing a grey film, blue thread veins becoming prominent over his body. It's only as he collapses, its muscles limp, do I notice the parallels between us again.

Another panel slides open from the next chamber with the now familiar hiss of steam drawing my attention from the debacle.

A swollen mass crashes wetly to the floor. Parts of what must be the abdomen fall away in translucent blobs of skin. Its appendages swollen and ill-formed, bulging eyes emerge from slits as he snorts into the air. I look away from the jellied sack, but the writhing slopping forces me to continue observations. Its cranium twists around as though it's a maggot trying to free itself from a lump of decaying flesh. The hair is wispy on the rear of its skull, leaving a ring of bare, transparent skin. Instinctively, I reach up, horrified to find the same thinning of hair. Even when the experiment goes wrong, there is something to learn.

The creature throws out a rubbery limb, its fingers squeaking against the flooring as it pulls itself forward, gurgling from froth corrupted lungs.

'Mine!' it rasps as it wriggles over its clothes. The bottle crunches under its mass, crackling like gravel embedding itself into the sluggish form. 'Mine.' It hisses as it continues to slither, a trial of blood smeared behind it.

My spine thumps against the solidness of the wall, my mind chasing after itself, locked into the nightmare as my footing slips away. I'm on top of something soft. A body. A corrupted version of myself. I push out against the clone I've fallen into. Its hand still rests on its now flaccid penis, fluid draining from its bowels in a dark, putrid stream. The head tilts forward against my own, as if sharing a whispered message. Its tongue pressed against my ear, the familiar stench, my own bitter odour overpowering me.

I lash out. Clawing, kicking, grabbing to be free of the thing. Only rolling closer to the globular mass, still slithering in a mess of organs. Its fingers wriggling worms reaching out.

'Mine.' Its teeth are a crooked collection of bones, a black chasm beyond.

The next station shunts open, hissing with the fever of dread and death. Possibly sensing the temperature surge, the jellied clone changes direction, hands slapping the ground, writhing and twisting towards the opening pod.

My palm is over my mouth, my diaphragm contracting painfully as I retch, not wanting to face any more of the abominations. And yet, I still focus on the open cloning booth. I watch the monstrosity flop closer, its neck twisting a bulbous head over the lip of the containment unit, mouth opening and closing pathetically.

'Mine' it gasps at the unseen thing inside just as the light fades to black.

The darkness doesn't last for long. Once the final pod has opened, the emergence indicator cuts off. The old fluorescent tubing fire overhead, elongated bulbs clanging internally as they start. In that moment, I realise the folly. Not of the experiment, but of failing to take control.

A clone steps out, over the writhing head and stops in front of the clothes now crumpled next to the thing still twitching against his feet, while the vial tinkles gently. He looks at me, although I know he is taking in the experiment's state. I click the pen frantically as I get to my feet.

'I'll need to drink this to help regulate my body.' His voice is without emotion. He stoops over and picks up the vial, unstoppering it and swigging it down. The veins along his throat stand out, his chest muscles are more pronounced on his slender frame. I wonder if this is a more accurate interpretation of my body. 'There have been corruptions in the process.' He says pulling on his clothes and glaring at me as he does so. At first I'm surprised, but then again, why should I be. The clone units restore from the last point of memory upload. If the mental capacity is there for them to accept the memory, then they should be capable of understanding the process. He throws the glass bottle where it shatters into fragments.

The creation at his feet jerks at the sound, but it's partly caught against the pod, unable to free itself.

'Mine!' it splutters, the word amplified by the hollowness of the chamber.

'Disgusting.' The now clothed clone says. The anger engulfs his face. He seizes the head of the creature, pulling it up to peer at its features. 'He doesn't even look like me.' He says before smashing the skull of the creature into the cloning booth. Again and again, he lifts and smashes the creature. The cracking replaced by damp thuds as bits of the skull peel open, skin sticking to the metal outer rim of the frame.

'Stop,' I mumble. The thing on the floor isn't moving, while the other me pauses, a smile across his bloodied face.

'What did you say?' He stands and brings the heel of his foot down against the hideous failure, once, twice. I can stand it no longer.

As I reach him, I realise too late he is ready. Perhaps his frenzied assault is a plan to create this response. His hands are steel chords around my neck.

'Don't,' I struggle. His strength knocks me. I fall heavily to the ground as he approaches, blood against his trousers, sleeves, teeth as he snarls. I raise my hands over my head, the pen pointing at him like a weapon.
'I'm collecting the data,', I scream. It seems pathetic, worthless, but yet he falters, connecting to my experiment, our experiment.

I feel my cheeks flushing with embarrassment at the way I'd let everything get out of hand. I must take charge.

The clone clenches his fists. Red droplets of blood around his flaring nostrils and the perfect white of his teeth.

We stand face to face. The pen heavy in my palm.

'Collecting data,' he says. His voice a perfect mockery of my own. Before I can stop him, he has moved to the table, pushing at the ordered collection of equipment. His finger rests on a passage in the notebook. The one I should never have underlined.

'The notes say we are only looking for one viable candidate.' He says, spinning back to me, a triumphant glow, his arms outstretched, unable to stop me thrusting the pen into his the deep brown of his eye.

When it's over, I'm gasping so hard, I don't notice the clunking locks to the door until it's opening.

A man is in the doorway, faded jeans and greying stubble. His eyes are blurry, still full of sleep, but there is no doubting the resemblance between this man and the failed experiments.

'Fucking clones,' he says, before raising the gun and pointing it in my direction.

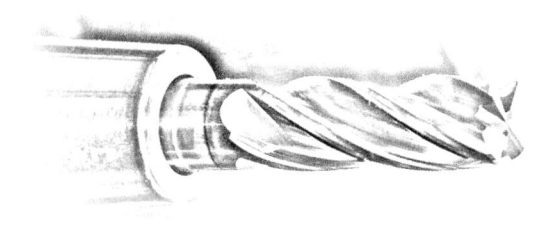

THE KRONOS

"You don't understand. I know I can stop it before it's too late. It's why I'm here. How many times do I have to say the same damn thing! You're not listening! I know more about all of this than anyone." I raised my head to the ceiling—the recessed bulbs, bright and burning against my eyes.

I'd watched hundreds of television shows with incompetent cops in the past. It was a cliché. I always thought it was lazy screenwriting, but here they were in the flesh. Officious, bureaucratic idiots who were impeding the hero, for real! They were more concerned in triple signing statements than doing anything to prevent further death. They left me to wait while they blundered from question to question, their footprints leaving a bloody, confused trail.

"I would like you to tell your story one more time if you don't mind, William?" He adjusted his posture. It surprised me he should attempt to sit up even more upright. He gave the impression of being pinned to one of those spinal injury boards, and at any moment, without the bonds, he would collapse.

I sighed, rolling my eyes dramatically, but nodded nevertheless. It was only when I cleared my throat that tears fell. They took me by surprise. I began gasping for air against the coiled up memories, and the helpless frustration they created. The second Detective, the one who had only just arrived, made to reach over with some tissues, but then changed his mind, holding them just in front of himself without purpose.

"I know we've covered a lot already, but can we start at the beginning?" He exchanged a glance at the other man, who had slipped his pack of tissues back in his pocket and was compressing a large folder into his chest. It was clear the guy had no stomach to hear the beginning of Kronos. Strangely, this idea only made me want to test his constitution, so I missed out on nothing.

I told them how I had 'found' a dead robin when I was fourteen, how I had concealed it in my schoolbag and taken it to my room. It felt so fragile, so light in my hands, and when I laid it on the bare skin of my chest, it belonged. Only it wasn't dead. Its little heart was a tiny quickening flutter against my own. On that day, I'd done something incredible, or so I thought. Through my will, I had created new life.

The man with the folder stopped me.

"Do we need to go back as far as this, William? Is it important to the monster?"

"Well, that's when it all started!" The room was too warm. I shifted in my seat, clenching and unclenching my fists, which drew their attention. It's deeply unpleasant being observed. I wondered how Kronos must be feeling to have the eyes of the world turned against him.

"Look at this picture, William." He slid the image across the table, the paper shifting with a glossy skid across the surface. The Detective's fingers pulled away from the picture as though it was on fire. Neither of them looked down themselves, both turning their heads until I picked it up.

They had taken the photograph from a high angle, some distance back at the corner of Kronos' cave. They must have used a drone or used some of my scaffolds; stalagmites hung next to the lens, half obscuring the sleeping giant, its skin a patchwork fusion. So many heads layered against each other to form eye sockets, putrified jelly at the centre, a thousand eyes to create the one.

"It's important that we all agree we are talking about the same thing here. Please confirm we are all on the same page, William? I can't see how the bird has any connection to this thing."

"His name is Kronos," I say. My voice calm against my unseen bubbling. "You must listen to me. The bird is the key to it all; it beats at the centre of Kronos, keeping it moving, hunting, absorbing people." I turn my head towards the vast mirror in the interview room. It reflects back at me. "That's why the beginning is important. It's not my fault." It felt more like a confession.

"Please, William. Tell us how this, Kronos, came to be."
I give the best account I can. How the robin took the cat, the very next day, feathers sinking into the fur on the back

of its body, its little wings twitching while the cat hissed and scratched. Then eventually it stopped making a fuss. The two were together. That's how they remained. I stare at the standing Detective, his skin grew pale and then green, especially when I explain how the animals became weaved together, becoming one.

The Detective with the folder fiddled with some of his papers. I could see he was distancing himself from my words. I repeatedly bash the tips of my shoes against the floor, my toes crunching. The Detective opposite, the one who hadn't reacted, his face as still as stone, leant towards me.

"Didn't anybody notice? Didn't family members, friends or even neighbours comment on the unusual anatomy of the cat?"

"I didn't let anybody see." I think I bared my teeth. "They wouldn't understand. I had to keep her hidden until…"

All the detectives did was slow things down. If they only listened. Their questions span around me like the twisted metal of a drill bit biting into bone. I should have been helping to stop Kronos before there is no stopping him.

"How long, before somebody spotted this creature, William?"
Some details are unimportant. I don't tell them about the thirst of my little robin, or how it needed more all the time. Neither did I mention how messy it was to see the first human join. Instead, I jump ahead.

"My mother," I say. "She came across us playing. It horrified her. There was no way for her to understand it. I asked her to leave well alone, but she couldn't and then she was a part of it too. It's a shocking thing to see when you're eighteen."

"Our records show that your mother, father and little sister lived at the same address, but there are no records of them over the last ten years." He looked at me; his eyes narrowed slits of anger.

My belly ached by the time I'd finished laughing. The years I'd carried around the guilt, blamed myself for their absorption, but all I'd done was help a bird's heartbeat. There was no point in them pushing their lack of understanding or guilt on me.

"I tried to stop it," I say. There had been a long silence after my convulsions, the last of my merriment faded slowly. They both look back up at me. "I thought about burning the house down with us still inside. I didn't. I wouldn't. Not with their eyes pleading, their mouths gasping, united in their efforts to communicate. That's why. So I waited until night and hid my family away, in a place they would never harm or be harmed."

"It didn't work out like that, did it?" The standing Detective had another photo ready for me. His rigid body poised on the edge of himself.

I smashed my hand against the table.

"No!" I shouted. "Kronos grew in the cave. Even though I'd hidden him well, secured him with chains, he still attached himself to others. The odd walker here, the stray animal there. It was never enough for Kronos."

"How many bodies?" The standing Detective's raised voice asked.

"Help me stop this before Kronos takes more. When he wakes, there will be no stopping him. Not without me." Why were they wasting so much time? I ground my teeth until my jaw ached. He repeated the question more forcibly, his lips moving mechanically. Over and over and over and over. "It's a simple question, William."

Kronos' infinite appetite were the stars beyond space. How could I even find the words?

I'd never intended to go back to that cave, but I did. At first every few months, towards the end, I hardly left. Why should I, when the creature you had given life to had grown magnificently? Each finger a human torso, tipped with polished bone and hundreds of tiny fingernails, like scales of a fish, shimmering in my torchlight.

They pushed another picture across the table. It was the burnt-out skeleton of a school bus.

"Do you recognise this?" He asked. I knew what it was, of course. I'm sure anybody around these parts would. It made the front page for months. "To clarify, this is the Castro Falls High School Bus. Just before Christmas, seven years ago, twenty-six students and the driver went missing. Continuous searching and a tremendous amount of investigative work revealed nothing. A terrible accident, terrorism, mass suicide, I've followed all scenarios. The school bus turned up four years ago at the bottom of an abandoned quarry. No bodies were remaining. Just the burnt-out husk. The media speculated that after this time animals had taken the corpses."

He paused, preparing another picture from his collection.
"I find it hard to believe. Animals or no." He took the photo he had been holding and moved it closer. It was another shot of the Kronos, this time of its left side, just under his putrefying arm.

"Have a good look at the photograph, William. You've see

the torn fabric in that section? The decomposing bodies, woven together, wear the Castro Fall's uniform..." He closed his eyes, fingers rubbing the darkened skin around them. "It is a little confusing how these bodies became infused with your creature when I investigated a school bus hundreds of miles away?"

He gestures to the large mirror. A few moments later, the door to the interview room opens. Uniform police officers stand on the other side, crammed into the narrow corridor, craning their necks, a rich tapestry of fear. The officer hands a clear bag with something heavy inside to the Detective.

"Do you know we are having difficulty with this? Not because of the dangers of your monster, but because it's so difficult to get somebody to want to study this thing. Its size indicates that there must be hundreds of bodies fused to create such a beast. How did that happen, William? That's what we want an answer on."

"You don't understand. It's going to get out of control unless you let me help you," I repeated, knowing that we were stuck in a meaningless cycle unless I could make them see.

"Do you know how many people suddenly disappear each year, leaving their children, the husbands, wives, parents, friends, pets, everything behind? They disappear without a trace." He slams his open palm down. "Gone! Some taken on their way home from work. Others after playing in the park. Do you know how many times I've had to tell parents of a missing children that there is nothing more we can do? Well do you?" I meet his stare full on. He breathes deeply. "I wonder how many we'll find in your Kronos?" I noticed his eyes watered.

The standing Detective placed the clear plastic bag on the table. My drill suspended inside, red smears against the corner of the bag where the spiralled metal rested.

"You recognise this?"

Even through the plastic, I could inhale Kronos. The damp, acrid, rotting of his lair forced my heart's rhythm to soar. The exploding decay across my face as screws twist against bones, tightening, securing through fleshy mounds, smothered me. I smile as if the blood splattered against my lips. It filled me with his voice as I screamed.

"Kronos will never stop. You must see this!" but, it is only my voice emerging.

"I think it is you, William, who doesn't understand. The only way I can stop this is by making sure you never see the light of day again. You have, over many years, slaughtered your own family. You've hunted and killed so many for your sick project, murdering people on mass. Such is your obsession. I can't imagine the lengths you have gone to in procuring your materials."

I looked at him blankly. They still didn't understand what would happen when Kronos woke. What will happen if I'm not there!

"I think I've already stopped Kronos, William. It's over."

The tiny wings stopped fluttering against my chest.

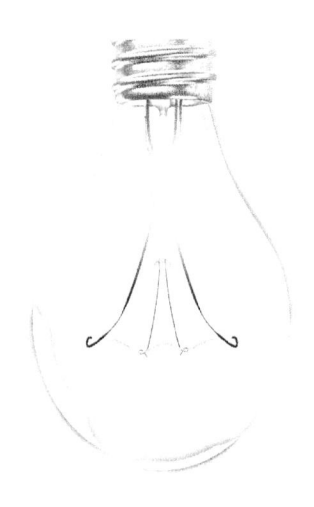

THE OLD MAN

"I don't see any point carrying on with the assessment, Mr Flynn. She is becoming distressed." The Doctor glanced at his notes. His wrinkle-free skin and smooth black hair reminded the son of his own kids, only without the awkward stance and their half-finished sentences. Instead, the Doctor's confidence emanated with his every movement, sitting in the air like expensive cologne.

"How long has she been like this?" the Doctor asked.

The son looked at his mother. She sat, shuffling scraps of paper around on the table, her body bent towards them, mumbling to herself as she placed them in groups before feverishly rearranging them into a different pattern as if they were part of a puzzle she couldn't solve.

"I don't live locally," the son said, "I have a house near the Cotswolds." He added, but immediately wondered why he had added anything at all. "There's been a distance…" The Doctor looked at the collection of notes he held and clicked his pen as if this was the last piece of punctuation. "We haven't seen each other for a very long time." The Doctor nodded as though agreeing with the statement. The son's cheeks flushed in the pause that followed.

"She has been brought here, Mr Flynn, because she cannot care for herself. In the records we have, there is nobody else. Your mother has you registered as the next of kin. My recommendation is that she stays until her assessment is complete, and we find a more suitable placement." The statement suspended itself. The son bit his lip. After he received the phone call, he'd prepared questions, lining them up like bricks in a wall, but now struggled with the foundations of any thought. The Doctor used the silence to place his pen between the folds of fabric in his breast pocket. A slither of silver, possibly a gift from his parents, slid away.

"Your mother needs twenty-four-hour supervision that the majority of families can't provide." Again, the Doctor paused. A swollen, expectant emptiness the son had no choice but to accept. "It rather upset her at being brought here. You should reassure her before you go." He smiled thinly. The Doctor's youthful brown eyes looked into the sons, holding him in place. "I have this for you. It gives useful advice, in case there is something that comes to you later on. There are forms you will need to sign at reception." The Doctor unzipped a black leather folder and pulled out a crisp leaflet.

"What should I tell her?" The son asked.

Cloud cover from outside caused the light through the barred windows to falter; the room darkened into a deeper shade of grey. All three of them looked towards the window as it lightened once more, their faces locked in a snapshot. Everything stood still for the briefest of moments until the mother moved again.

"Mr Flynn, I can't advise on these things." The Doctor looked back at the mother and then at the son. Pressure squeezed against his body. "Usually, the family constructs a story that fits the narrative. That is to say; they feed the delusion to minimise any sense of worry for the patient. The patient's family often knows what is best." The Doctor picked his coat off the corner of the bed. He cleared his throat. A prolonged cackling of dryness. "A typical family stays with the patient as long as they need them to." That final pen click. The son said nothing.

When they were alone, the son watched his mother. He looked on his phone, wondering if there was somebody to call. When he looked back at his mother, she had removed the scraps of paper from the table and was clutching them in a bony, blue talon.

"Mum," he tried. His words belonged to a boy from the past and not the man who stood in the doorway. His mother looked up at him, and her face lit up. The son relaxed, a warmth spreading through him.

"Darling, why are you out of bed? Your father won't be happy. You know what the old man can be sometimes. Don't let him catch you. Not like the others!" She swivelled her thin body around on the small armchair, the kind with wooden armrests which often populated clinical settings. "Don't be too hard on the boy, Syd. You know how scared he gets sometimes." He looked towards the space his mother spoke into.

"Mother, it's been a few years since..." He stopped himself. "He's not here." Aged muscles in her face sagged, forcing her loose skin into thick wrinkles. Her emptiness expanded in his chest—a tightening he needed to control.

"He will be back soon, though, don't worry."

"I told you never to come back here, you little shit! Not after you ran off. That's your problem. Too scared to face the truth. Too scared to stay." The son recognised a past across her face, the veins standing out solid against her neck. Her words, her movements, her memory, too solid to be real. "Where's Syd?" The distress overpowered her. His mother's sudden change pulled at his breath, catching his words; an emptiness washed through him, pulling him back from the light into a darkened corner. His chest tightened so rapidly; it hurt to push out his words.

"I'll go get him now. Why don't you rest while I fetch him?" The mother looked at him, her eyes inky pits against her yellow skin, and then to his surprise, she reached out her hand. Her skin was softer than he thought, her palms warm and delicate. He helped her into the bed, pulling the thin, blue sheets across her scrawny body. A mild scent of urine made him struggle with the stranger in his arms. "I'll ask somebody to lower this for you, mum."

"Make sure my Syd doesn't catch you sneaking around our house. You know the old man has a temper. Don't let him catch you up to no good, not like last time." Her face distorted into a grimace, teeth bared, with no sound at first, but then the croaking came. It clicked against the moisture at the back of her throat, building in volume into a cruelness he didn't want, a callousness he had buried long ago. His legs sank into the ground with each stumbled step away. Her laughter slowed as she rested herself flat on the bed before stopping. The stillness of his mother's body made him shiver.

The solidness of the closed door pressed back against him as he steadied his breathing. The knots in his chest unwound and the pain with it. He inhaled, pushing the air out into the sterile white corridor around him. At the far end, he noticed a withered man watching, hair wild, body frail, as still as a sculpture. The son walked the other way towards reception.

* * *

Instead of going straight into the house, he sat in the driveway looking through the leaflet. Skimming through the lines of text in the fading light, he tried his best to absorb the information. Very little made any sense. Words swirled around, colliding with each other as he wrestled with the idea of travelling home instead. This allowed him comfort. Kathryn would rub his arm and embrace him, as they discussed everything with a detached calmness. As much as he wanted to, there wasn't any point in driving three hours there and having to come back in the morning. Of course, it would be just one night. He could get a lot sorted in one push, look through paperwork, get the things she might need for her ongoing stay at a nursing home and deliver it first thing in the morning. The selling of the house and emptying its contents, he intended to organise at a later stage, getting others to do the bulk of this for him. One night, and he would never have to come back.

From the driver's seat, he observed the overgrown rose bushes, the shabby hedges and the paint peeling from window frames, revealing spots of rot. These details were the same as he had always remembered, only disconnected by his absence. They reflected a change that jumped through decades, but as the details of the house soaked into him, he became unsure if they hadn't always been that way.

Finally, he made his mind up. Hitting the steering wheel a few times with the palm of his hand, the same way that a boxer may slap his chest to ready himself before a fight, he walked to the front door. The keys he had chinked like chains as he tried one and then moved onto the next. There were so many of varying sizes, the twisted fingers of a skeleton, each one cold and dead in his grip. One clicked into place, allowing him to push open the door.

The scent made him turn his head in disgust. A combination weaved in and out of detection, enveloping, overpowering as he recognised the heavy odour of damp. It clung to the back of his throat, making him gag. It forced him to cover his mouth. Reluctantly, he closed the front door, throwing himself into the sickly gloom. The son's hands groped across the wall, fingers whispered across the embossed paper in search of a light switch that no longer was where he had just observed it to be. The darkness pressed at his vision, a maladaptation forcing away his sight. He sank into the depths, struggling for air. In the tenebrific hallway, on his own, the walls, the floors, even the ceiling contracted. A ticking clock became the choking, spasming, involuntary gasp for air. The son, for just a moment, struggled to breathe, the floor tightening against his feet. He was the lump lodged in the throat of a monster. Still, he searched, reaching low and then high, his hand a drowning wave. Then he found it. With a click of the switch, he illuminated the hallway. He came up for air, a sweat settled against his forehead and a segment of himself clicked into place.

There was no instant familiarity, not in the way he had expected. Despite this, the discomfort made him reach back for the door. Coats crowded onto the stand, like bodies embracing one another. A large shirt hung, half undone, its arms rolled up, giving an appearance of being only just removed. A half-open bag had fallen over, spilling the contents of life onto the ground. His mother's worn shoes, with their dirty yellow insoles half hanging out, were next to the wall. One was further back than the other; they looked as if somebody had stepped out mid-stride and disintegrated into the brickwork. The hallway had wallpaper, which in probability would have been up thirty years ago when he had lived in the house. He couldn't remember, its pattern and colour so hideous it embedded itself with a lasting impression from a mere medusa glance. Neither his mother nor father had thought to replace any part of the decoration. Instead, the years had faded the paint and worn grooves in the linoleum flooring, tracing their passage and the son's absence. But now only he remained, outlasting them, returning as the man of the house.

Eventually, he took his hand off the door and moved onwards into the scent of the house. A further distraction that kept his conscious away from the nagging at the back of his mind. He covered his nose with the back of his hand, hoping it would dissipate, although a part of himself, an irrational faction, was fearful. Instead, he imagined ingesting the sourness, so it leaked through the cracks in his pores, always.

Pictures lined the wall opposite the stairway. He leant into the grainy black and white images from the past. Despite being abandoned in time, a prisoner in his parents' clutches, little faces called out to him. In the centre sat a grainy image of a wedding day. Two figures strode towards the camera while pieces of confetti hung frozen in the air. As he leant in closer to the image, the obscurity of their faces was apparent. Any distinctness of nose, mouth or shape faded into brightness. He absorbed the images. They sat on the precipice, each one fitting into place once he had taken a moment of exploration. A picture of his mother throwing a ball to his brother and himself caught his attention; they were smiling. He wished to remember that day or recollection of the time before his little brother had died. A photo teased him with a possibility of something that didn't exist. A big brother was smiling, his hands raised. The blond curly hair, so different from the lacklustre, age stricken mess his locks had become. What were the dreams of those in the photographs? Did they ever imagine themselves held in place while a future searched them for meaning? None of the photographs, apart from his parents getting married, had his father captured in them. It took him a few moments to realise why.

An urge filled him, as it did most evenings. The desire to let things flow past him with the richness of alcohol. He passed the wall of photos and tried the door to where he knew the kitchen to be.

The room had a faint blue glow from the old upright hob where spewing gas gave its disapproving hiss. He raced over, shaking his head at the negligence of those who must have carted his mother away. The rest of the kitchen was in disarray, clean but disordered with a strangeness which disturbed him. Cutlery lay across the kitchen surface, arranged next to each other like the fossils of an ancient creature pieced together. In the sink, his mother had left a punnet of tomatoes, ripe and red against the silver. Maybe it had made sense to her fading brain, an order in chaos.

The wine, as he had expected, sat in the pantry's corner. There were bottles of red, white, whiskey, and brandy. Greasy dust covered them, which stuck to his fingers as he browsed his cellar. He selected a red, uncorked it and poured its contents into a plastic beaker which sat on the draining board. That first swig fired his insides, the liquid tracing a passage deep within, relaxing him. The richness spilt over his lips. He was no longer a child, but a man taking over the responsibilities of the family. A strange thought occurred to him. He had always been right. This wine, his freedom of the house, that his mother needed him now was the evidence. He poured himself another beaker while looking at the cracks across the ceiling and the faded tiles. He needed to get a sense of order again. Scooping up the tomatoes, he pulled open the fridge and jumped back.

It lept towards him from the bowels of the refrigerator, diving at his head and shoulders, twisting into his form before crumpling into the inanimate objects it had always been. The son stepped back, mouth agape as more of the contents rattled to the ground. Chaos spread as thick wads of glossy white paper slid across the kitchen floor; canisters rattled and rolled against his feet, old-style camera film unravelled into arks of brown translucent strips, open tin cans rattled, their contents spilling into the heap. He brushed at his clothes, stepping on the greying papers as he backed away. They darkened further, blackening from the exposure, the supernatural presence of science. The son kicked at one can, the fuzzy mould flourishing around its rim, while its serrated silver tongue wobbled as it bounced across the kitchen. He lent to pick up the changing paper. He held it, a lost part of his childhood returned. Unfixed, the once white photographic sheet was now black in his hands. The decay surrounded him, filling the kitchen, forcing him to pull his head away from the mass and make his escape.

Back in the hallway, he calmed with a few more swigs of wine before emptying the bottle. His phone vibrated in his pocket. Kathryn's name lit up the screen.

"Hi," his words sluggish as they left his mouth.

"Is everything okay? We've been waiting to hear from you." Her voice so far away. "Did you speak to your mum? What did the Doctor say?"

"I've decided to stay the night while I sort things out. She has moved to a temporary home for an assessment."

"What does that mean? How sick is she?"

"She has advanced dementia." The words tripped him.

"Are you okay? I'm so sorry, darling. Did you speak to her?" The phone crackled, her voice distorted, merging into electronic pulses.

"Kat? I think the phone is cutting out?" Static screamed from the receiver, the odd word, a sharp screech, then her voice again, but this time with a higher pitch, more frantic. "Kat - you there?"

"What do you mean? Your father's dead. I know you're upset about everything, and maybe you expected none of this, but he died two years ago. I just don't see your point." She paused; he tried to catch up with what she had said, grasping at the missing conversation.

"I'm not sure what you mean, Kat. I think you must have misheard me."

"No, you were clear. You are not your father and never have been. I want you to know that. Okay? He is not inside you!" That same uncomfortable pressure pushed against him once more, squeezing like he was deep underwater.

"Kat," he began, his words emerging cautiously, "I've not mentioned my father on the call." The line crackled again. "What do you think I said, Kat?"

"Are you drinking?" The words buzzed at him, distorting her humanity as her voice burnt into his ear.

"Look it's been difficult. It's been the first time I've seen my mother; she is still the nasty piece of work I remember." Again, the phone signal became distorted, screeching as he pulled the handset from his ear before her panicked voice returned.

"Get out of there now!"

"What, Kat?"

"If you've seen somebody in the house, get out now! Call the police and get out!"

"What are you saying, Kat? I've not said anything of the sort. We must have a crossed line. Kat?"

"You're breaking up. The reception is cutting out." She said. He walked closer to the front door, calling into the phone as he went.

"Hello. I'm talking. Hello?" He stood by the front door. Her voice, so tinny and far away, struggling to get through to him.

The line went dead. The screen's light faded to an electronic blackness.

He only noticed the hushed slip of card against card after he had finished staring at the blank screen. Holding his head up, he listened, hoping there was nothing, but there it was, the unmistakable sorting slip of photographs shuffling against themselves. His face hardened, and he moved his ear closer to the door, his mind desperate to find an explanation.

He pushed at the door to the lounge. It moved inward, before crashing closed against the son. The sound of paper scraping both intensified in speed and volume, matching his rising pulse. Reaching out again, he tried the door. It resisted. His entire body tingled with a sense of unreality, of not touching the floor or the handle, yet the metal was in his palm. His polished shoes sat against the frayed brown carpet which crept underneath the threshold from the living room. A faded image from the past, his own experiences eroded his mother and his father and the house. The partly remembered ideas of living here, the ones he had shared with Kathryn, struggled against the boundaries he had imposed on them. With each passing moment inside, the fluidity of the past became part of him, clarifying, focusing on the things he kept locked away.

He put more force behind the door. The metal hinges worked to announce his intention, but it still resisted, pushing back at him, fighting him. He didn't stop; he didn't turn away, not this time, not as before. Even though he realised the better part of him willed him to let go, never to get inside. Finally, it gave. The pressure holding it closed weakened, allowing the son just enough of the hallway's light to slide through the gap. The room revealed the outline of the empty couch by the window—next to the small coffee table. Minor pieces of white were visible on its surface. Still, he heard the rustling and the sound of his heart hammering. He heaved against the door. It flew back, crashing against an unseen object, revealing the room in full and the dark shape of the old man's chair. In the gloom, the high outline of the backrest formed a menacing shape.

The sound was distinct, not the smooth sliding hush of paper, but the cracking movement of the leather armchair. It groaned and creaked as if through the weight of a body. In the half-light, dismissed by his rational brain, he thought he caught sight of a movement pulling back into the darkest recess of the chair.

"Who's there?" He said, his voice a feeble cloud caught in the sudden chill of the room, translucent mist gathering around his mouth.

He flicked the light switch, exposing the emptiness. Positioned, next to the fireplace, sat his father's chair. Although the room was unfamiliar, there was something about the old man's chair, as they had called it, which made him wonder how he had ever forgotten this detail. Continual wear had created cracked armrests where elbows had gnawed, the white interior showing through like broken skin revealing fresh growth. Signs of the former occupant clung to the seat; the indentation more than an absence of human flesh, but part of the meat. A curve of legs, the hollow of an elbow, the concave of his father's head engraved in its place. The son leaned in closer to the creased leather as the indentations lifted, fading with relief. A density crushed him, of childhood nightmares, of sweat-soaked fevers, filling him, forcing him to drown in the forgotten.

"Father?" His voice was little more than a choked whisper. The empty room didn't respond. The complete silence interrupted by the rapid buzzing movement of a fly which repeatedly threw its body at the light bulb, creating a tiny tinkering against the glass.

If it had happened slower, or he was in a less heightened state, he might have hung onto seeing something disappear into the old man's chair. For the briefest of moments, in the near darkness, he was sure an arm had vanished into the leather skin of the battered object.

The son pulled away, his legs knocked at the coffee table. Across the surface, little pieces of squared glossy paper, their tiny ragged edges standing out against the dark wood, shimmered, lifting, travelling by the force of invisible fingers just off the tabletop. He tried to stop it, but his stomach lurched, turning with a plummeting roller coaster of burden. With a trembling slowness, he reached for a scrap, he realised they were sitting in clear liquid. The lip around the edge was just high enough to prevent it seeping to the floor. The substance displaced as he picked up one of the glossy squares, the stickiness and chemical aroma, creating even more discomfort. His nose wrinkled with the faint acidic odour which caught him.

The small paper in his hand changed, not fading to black this time, but an image forming against the white background. Across the table surface, the scraps developing, ghostly faces appearing from their shallow resting places. Tiny eyes stared back at him from the table, becoming more apparent as though a mist. Curls of hair emerged, along with a melancholy expression he recognised. It was a child. Could it be him?

The settee's cushions folded against his legs as he collapsed onto the surface. The leather of the old man's chair groaned with the fading impressions while the face continued to develop on the little slip he held in his hand, thoughts juggling with impossibilities. *It was the change in temperature he created when opening the door. He had disturbed the chemicals, causing the pictures to develop.* All of his explanations constructed a plausibility. But no matter how he convinced himself, his imagination continued to suggest a presence watching him from the old man's chair. His hands tensed, one squeezing the tumbler until it twisted out of shape, the other screwing the tiny image he still held in his fist.

The son raised his drink. "Here's to you, Father." The words struggled out against the wine. He cleared his throat if only to stop the noise of the flies expanding buzz. "You never knew me." The son took a big slurp, contents spilling onto his shirt where it spread out with ragged fingered edges around his neck. "I only found out today, so I guess I'm in mourning. Not that I can say I knew you. Then again, you never knew me did you, Father." His words battled against the flies' continuous momentum.

He poured more red into his cup, his teeth clenched. As days go, this was a tough one. At least Kathryn was waiting for him when he got home. For now, he needed to concentrate on getting things organised, gathering basics for his mother, finding the billing companies and dealing with everything he needed. There was nobody else to do it. This sense of reassurance calmed him, making him think of real-estate, estimating the cost of the house. The quicker he could organise things, the faster he could sell the dingy hovel and get out. He just needed to tie things up this time. He wasn't the frightened child who ran away.

The fly had lost interest in the illumination; instead, buzzing around the son's head, drawing his attention just as his eyes closed. It dived in towards his ear, unseen as it lingered with its resonating hum, before disappearing again. The son shifted on the couch, more alert. The rev of the creature moved up in intensity as it landed against the fabric of his clothes, the furniture, the tip of his ear before he jerked to send it on its way again. Just as he moved his lips to take another sip, the fly landed on the rim, dipping its front legs against the rich liquid clinging to the side of the plastic. It's black, translucent wings flicking against the beaker. He squirmed, pulling his hand back, knocking more wine across his chest and trousers.

"Shit, shit, shit." He said as he rested his drink on the table. The bottom of the cup catching and spilling across the surface, gathering at the ridges and pooling against the tiny images left in the chemical. Instinctively, he righted the tumbler and tried to pull the photographic paper to one side. There was no reason to save them, but he tried. The whole table turned a light red colour, wine adding to the chemical and pushing over the lip, so it dropped onto the carpet in thin drips, plopping with each fall. He tried to sweep the tide of red into the centre of the table only for it to pool again to another side, his hand and shirt covered by the wine as it gathered around the fabric of his wrists.

"Fuck! Shit! Fuck!" He pulled himself off the couch, the fly buzzing around his head, louder than it had ever been.

The wine clung against the fabric of his shirt, making it difficult to peel away from his skin, but once he had, the chill fell upon him with an icy touch. Involuntary shivers spread across his body as he stepped back out into the hallway and pulled the shirt from the stand. The thick chord material covered his body with an unfamiliar stiffness. Its fit was too big, the bottom dangling to his thighs, but it was dry. A staleness of developing fluid, awakened by the movement, rose out of the threads, swirling around him, pulling at those half-hidden memories. A jumble of images settled before misting over once again, leaving him with hollow pain. He couldn't remember any detail, just shouting, his father's power, watching the coat stand and the lingering of drying tears against his cheek.

The son shook his head, his face twisted in horror at the flood of thoughts which had been waiting for him in the house, hanging against every wall, ceiling, fitting or decoration. Every detail crowded him with the burden of his experience so it anchored him, pulling him under the depths, deeper and deeper, further and further, until he recalled the staircase, a creaking trap he had negotiated to escape on that night.

He pressed his foot against the bottom step, the wood groaned as he began his ascent. He took the next, avoiding the centre by pushing his feet to the far sides, a movement so ingrained in his memory from years ago, his body responded as automation. The boards against his feet remained silent. The ticking clock matched the beating of blood through arteries. The fly continued to buzz. The son tested the centre of the step, the leather sole pushing lightly, but yet the wood moaned against his weight. There was no way he could stop himself. Each onward step, slow against the nagging fear lurking inside, forcing adrenaline to build and with it, a compulsion to run. *Not this time.*

The buzzing grew as he continued into the gloom of the stairs, piercing him with each painful footfall. With his fingers against his ears, he kept climbing, until the meagre yellow bulb of the landing came into view. The uncovered light sent shadows from the bannister's runners, forming bars across the son's face as he looked beyond the stairs to the room he had once occupied.

It hung from the ceiling on a yellow strip next to the dust-covered bulb. As he stood at the top of the landing, drawn to the sight of the tiny creatures squirming against the sticky fly tape. There were so many of them, struggling as though one, a segmented pulsating creature, their wings, legs, parts of its exoskeleton and even heads left attached as they wrenched themselves free. The remains of their bodies falling to the floor underneath with a soft plopping sound. An infinite number of corpses rested against the surface of the carpet, tiny black spots forming a ragged circle of death which popped under the soles of his feet as he passed underneath. Still, they fell with agonising slowness, the soft pattern of invisible digits drumming to an irregular rhythm.

The room was empty, moonlight flooded against the walls. There were no curtains, just a mattress and a few pieces of ripped chord lying discarded. He rubbed his wrists, an unconscious pain in his crowded head. An empty existence, his, wiped clean from the house.

The next door must have been his brothers, only standing outside, his sibling was lost in time. It seemed essential to reconnect before he entered. A reluctance stalled his arm mid-reach. *Run before it's too late.* The son's hand rested against the door; he hoped this gave him a connection before he entered, as though mental images of his brother could reconnect them through time.

The room swallowed his breath. A small bed occupied the centre, an altar in a shrine. All around, overfilled shelves lined the walls. Hundreds of toys looked at him, unused, and still boxed. Many of the packages were covered with a thick layer of dust. Not all the toys dated back to his childhood. Instead, a numbness overcame him when he noticed the many recent additions squeezed onto the shelves. His insides clenched. He picked up a faded box with a plastic window, leaving a dust-free square where it had been sitting.

A little doll with blonde hair looked back at him, its eyes wide and unblinking with inanimate stillness. Everything about the cheap plastic doll made the hairs across his body tingle. Its place, part of a collection for an unknown purpose. He had entered a world so unfamiliar, a mother who was sick, and news of a dead father, but he didn't know either of them. They, this house, were strangers to him. There was no way to know who they had become after he left, and even what he could remember of being there was only just beginning to shift back into focus, but it wasn't enough for him to be sure. Through the hum of flies, the pained head, the creeping dread around him, he needed to know. A buried past laid in the house, and this was the key to himself, he was sure.

Pain forced his hand to his temple, pressure pounding against his skull. He closed the door to the bedroom. The light from the bulb was too intense, but he tightened his jaw and ignored his unsteady feet against the floor or the continuous painful buzzing against his ear. There were only two rooms he hadn't checked. The first of these was his parent's, knowledge of them clearer now, as though he had regained focus. The other door had always been a mystery. It had been out of bounds and policed by his father. Until this moment, standing only feet away, he had forgotten its existence.

As he always said, boundaries were important. Of course the office and the attic were out of bounds for their children as they were growing up, but this didn't mean they had never been in them. The son had never even seen inside; his father had the key hanging from a string around his neck.

The handle moved. He steadied himself to enter. The out-of-bounds room was locked.

He pushed his way into his parent's bedroom. The large wardrobe guarded the bed, as it always had. Its ornately carved top stood out like curled locks of hair. Even now, as an adult, it dominated him, making him want to turn. Pressing in further, the source of the flies became obvious. Their still bodies clinging to walls while others descended in jerking movements so quick, they were impossible to follow. Others bumped against the ceiling with a lightness, miniature overfilled balloons with nowhere to escape.

The musty atmosphere which pervaded the rest of the home intensified, catching at the back of his throat with each gasp of air. It was more than decades without airflow, decomposition draped itself across the ordered bedsheets and folded blankets. The bed looked unused, as though nobody had slept or even used the room for some time due to the visible dirt resting across the surfaces, sitting across the bedsheets and bedside tables in a powdery white layer. He turned back to leave.

A vast outline of a figure stood motionless behind the door, half-hidden by the folds of darkness. A glutinous, bulging being who leaned with its visible deformity. Its chest a barrel bursting forward while its legs swelled. A suggestion of a head slumped back into the body.

The son stood frozen against the shape, his will shaking inside his frame, but still, he couldn't move. An eternal moment passed in which the flies landed on the unmoving giant, and the darkness evolved the monster into nothing more than two black bin bags, stacked on top of each other. He pushed the mental image, saturating his intelligence away as he approached the sacks. He compressed one, the softness inside gave under his touch as the contents swelled, shifting against its thin restraint as though alive. Suddenly the bag above toppled, splitting open so that a mass of fabric tumbled to his feet. The son pulled back, aware as the plastic ripped at its seams, spilling its guts onto him. The arm and body of a small child's jacket wrapped itself around his leg while several other clothes scattered themselves into dishevelled bundles. He kicked at one. The clothes erupted into a tangled heap. Flies crawled out from between the creases. Their constant humming growing.

Kneeling, he pulled the layers of cloth apart. One item of clothing, followed by another, for both genders, emerged from the pile. He pulled his hands into the bags pulling out even more, ripped, soiled with grime, they poured from the slashes his hands had gouged in the thin black plastic. His nails caught against fabrics, knitted jumpers from his childhood to little nylon tracksuits of the last five years. He spread them out in front of him, with the weight of sudden understanding collapsing amongst the material.

He lay sobbing, his body falling onto his side and the keys he still had in his pocket pressing at him until his eyes hurt and the tears stopped flowing.

Mind exploding against the noise, he pulled himself towards the out-of-bounds room, keys in hand, eyes blurry. The keys fell through his fingers until one caught with its potential. The remains of string caught against the head of the key. From the internal workings of the door, he could hear the catch clicking free. His hand rested on the handle.

Black fabric hung across the doorway, so dark in their internal folds, it reached out from an absence of existence. He could still turn away, leave the house and never come back, but he knew he had gone beyond this now. He stepped into the curtain, pushing the material aside, letting the smothering darkness take him.

Wrapping his pounding head as if submerged, he stood in the beginning before creation, without body, only his fragmented thoughts confirming his existence. Willing movement, his head, his arms, there was no way of knowing in the absolute absence around him. He slid his foot forward, relieved of at least the connection with the ground. Again, he waved, stretching out to take hold of something, but found only himself. He turned to move back, reaching for the curtain, unsure of the direction he was facing. *Stay calm. Use the exercises.* He pulled at the air, breathing out with a rasping that wasn't his own. It was then he felt it against his neck—a sharp, delicate sensation, a fingernail drawn across his skin. There were no more tears from boyhood to shed. Despite this, he pushed back at his childhood, turning as the lightness of touch moved across his face. He closed his fingers around the end of a chord, a bulbous fastening in his palm, which he pulled.

Red light spilt across the walls and floors. The room was smaller than the void he had conjured, the vast darkness distorting his sensations, but now it was overcrowded, the pressure squeezing at him once again. To his side, he could see photos hanging on a wire. Behind this, images mounted onto the wall. He moved into them, his heart heaving, his legs shaking as he absorbed what he saw. Many were half-developed, but they were children. He recognised himself in many, playing football with another boy, his younger brother, but it wasn't just him. There were other children. His mother held two other boys in her arms or walked hand in hand with girls.

Next to the wall were three development trays and table space. He pushed his fingers into the red-stained liquid, chemicals rising to meet him. On the wall behind were more photographs, so many of different sizes. Huge, partially recognised portraits leered at him. Ahead, the walls narrowed into a corridor created with cheap boarding. The walls squeezed at him, twisting him on an onward course. Ducking around another red bulb hanging low from the ceiling, the son turned the corner. Space opened up, the red light reflecting against the large prints held in place. The first, a large portrait of a young boy, no older than six. The boy's blond curly hair, so similar to his own, sat on his head. He looked at the camera. The boy's eyes cast towards the ground. In scrawled handwriting, near the bottom was a date long in the past. Next to this was another face, one he didn't recognise with the same scrawled writing, and then another, and another. The son walked into the centre, spinning against the rows of faces staring back.

A movement caught his attention.

A large photograph, at the furthest part of the room, had moved. Instead of a pubescent boy, this image captured an old man looking back. The son could see the pale hair protruding around his head in a wild formation and the open whites of staring eyes. The mouth opened agape, displaying a never-ending abyss. The son could see no man, only a creature who had always chased him through his horrors.

The son turned, crashing into the wall, tearing against the images attached. Fetid breath grasped towards him. Rounding the corner, he looked back. The old man was moving closer, an arm's length apart, a monster everywhere. The son crashed past the hanging red light, catching himself on chords, everything pulling at him. An icy grip dragged at his throat while he clawed at nothing more than the crimson wash spilling around. The old man was against him, the past tumbled, whimpering children, hands tied, eyes watering as he passed by doors left ajar, heads turned up, his father's fists beating at a younger him until his brother didn't move.

Still, he thrashed out, pushing at the old man who was no

more than air. It was no use. He could feel whispering against his ear, the red-veined eyes next to his own, the grey skin stretching around his face until he couldn't scream out, but still he fought. The entity pulled at his form, twisting inside himself until his muscles burned but still he battled. The curtain grabbed at him, a fabric of fear imprisoning him.

He spilt onto the floor on the other side of the curtain, the black folds quivering. With wheezing breath, he pulled himself up, half expecting the curtain to pull back and hands claw him into the darkness beyond. The curtain remained still. He closed the door and struggled to get the key into the lock.

The door banged, bouncing in its frame with such anger that even the surrounding air reverberated. Again and again, it pushed at him, so he had to steady his hands against the beating wood.

Bang. Bang. Bang.

His fists flew against the door with such rage, pain pulsed through his arm.

Bang. Bang. Bang.

Silence.

He took a step back and then another until he was free. The house was still.
Steadily, he descended the staircase, each footstep cracked against the unseen timber underfoot. The exhaustion overwhelmed, although now there was a solution.

At the kitchen door, he watched the blue flame from the hob lick the surrounding air. The gas snaked towards him, ready to attack and consume the past until it no longer existed. The old man could sit and wait.

The leather creaked around him as he settled. His mind took flight, drifting through memories, like a man looking through a photo album. Hands rested against his brown shirt and the key to the dark room once again on a string necklace. His eyes closed.

BLACK FOX

Late afternoon, warm sunlight caressed the brim of his nose and brow as he angled to seize the last of its influence before it slipped out of sight behind the grand oak. In moments such as this, he missed smoking, resting in the backyard with a fresh carton of cigarettes and only the birds' voices to keep him company. That occasion of blissful contentment in which he interrupted the world and forced aside the bitterness, if only for a moment. Everything has a consequence. No matter how much he wanted to reverse the events of the past, he couldn't accomplish any of it, and any plans for the future faded like dissipating smoke from his damaged lungs.

The rear door from the conservatory creaked open, and

Jan appeared. Everything in him plummeted. Nevertheless, he smiled, not saying anything as she struggled down the high step onto the patio with a bottle of wine and two glasses. It pleased him to see the wine while a knot tightened in his throat at Jan's presence. Rob knew he should tell her, in the same clinical way he had been told, without any emotion or hope for a different outcome. It was his duty. Only, he hadn't found the right opportunity to face the rawness of it. Regardless of how polished his words, how well she took the information, those old bruises were still tender, and all the years between them would break apart.

Jan sat the chinking glasses down on the little round table, its paint clinging on in places, but not worth replacing. It did its job after all, and mostly that's enough.

"Could have given me a blooming hand," she said.

"Ay, I might have done, but where is the fun in that." Her face pouted and twisted with the usual mechanism, her lips protruding. He noticed she had put on makeup.

It took her a moment to unscrew the lid; she sighed with each effort, like an athlete set to take on a feat of strength. Again, he didn't offer to help. He folded his arms at the cheap paper logo stuck lopsidedly onto the bottle. He remembered the days of popping corks and making love as the bubbles dribbled across her firm form. Now, the contours of her naked body were a mystery. The best of those days gone, leaving behind the sound of the heavy red as it glugged into mismatched glasses, their routine a rut carved in the mud. She sipped noisily. He didn't grimace, just let it all fade away into the breeze which swayed against the hedgerow's ragged tops.

A butterfly, so delicate, cascaded end over end, dancing above the neat lawn, an intricate piece of silk pulled on a magician's wire before it settled in the middle of a sunflower. Its wings opened and closed a few times, an eye blinking with happiness.

"Did you hear about Maurice?" The butterfly skittered up into the sky. Rob watched it flutter away wistfully; he didn't adjust the smile on his face, painted on by years of experience. Instead, he picked up his glass, the tiny amount she poured him swirling around at the bottom, deep, rich with flakes, like small slithers of bark, he hoped was the mark of the brand.

"Stroke, they say. Can you believe it? He was very active. When I spoke to Anne, she said that was his problem, constantly up to mischief, not able to settle, not for five minutes, even in the evening. He had his hobbies, not anything important, things to busy himself with, painting and military writing about this war or the next. Anne didn't know what Maurice was up to most of the time. I said you were the same, mostly off busy with one thing or another. Last Christmas he'd requested a metal detector. Anne told me he insisted on having it. She didn't get it, of course, not with his heart. Can you imagine him out on his own in some field, and then he's on all fours gasping in the dirt? Well, I said to her, it would have been a waste and with the world as it is, who has that kind of money to throw away. Not these days, at any rate. What was he expecting to find? That's what I asked her. We did chuckle."

She waited, always had. He saw the yearning for more, a part of him she'd never given up hope on. He felt exhausted with the weight of the conversation, her expectation of him to continue being the man she had first married. Even after all those years in which the distance widened.

The pause between them grew stale. Only the short, high chirps of two birds called out to each other. Rob watched as first one, then the other sparrow, darted into a gap in the ferns, each holding thin, twisted twigs in their beaks. A little late in the year to be raising young, he thought. Their tiny bodies a blur of motion, he wondered how they made their way with such precision into the slight gap they had created. Life would continue. After he was gone, the sun would still rise, the seasons would change.

Jan shifted in her seat with mild discomfort, caught in shadows, direct sunlight hidden from them. She ran her thumb along the prominent rim of the glass, lost in her thoughts.

"Is he okay?" Rob asked. He couldn't remember if he'd ever met Maurice. Not that he'd ever bothered with any of Jan's friends. She had a great many to keep track of, enough for both of them. Rob had lost touch with his own. Not returning their calls, not wanting to listen to them as they struggled with condolences. The years had passed into decades, and the memory of them faded. Old wounds only festered if they weren't closed.

"Well, they had to make a complaint at the hospital not long after he was there. They should have gone private, not with the hospitals as they are and all those diseases. It's enough to put you off getting ill if you ask me. Apparently, they hadn't given him a meal the second day. Of course, it didn't matter because Anne had taken some of her homemade sandwiches with her. The ones with that nice chutney she does. Well, she made the complaint, and now she has to go through official channels. Can you believe it?"

Rob prepared what he needed to say..

"So, I said to her..."

Rob leaned forward, craning his neck. A dull ache filled his lower abdomen, spreading up and pushing at his lungs. This, he was used to. It was the jet black fur sticking out from the ferns at the end of the garden which had caught his attention.

He held up a hand. Jan's eyes bloated. Rob pointed over in the direction of the parting foliage as a head emerged. A long snout, the colour of coal, pushed free of the green leaves. Two large pointed ears, tipped with splashes of white, flicked around independently of each other. Jan had seen it too, resting her glass on the table as she looked from the animal to Rob and then back to the creature. It continued toward the lawn, its sleek tail balancing behind it. It was a giant cat, more the size of a large dog. No, not a domesticated animal. It was a large black fox. The fox sniffed at the ground in front of it, taking a few tentative steps out into the open. Jan grasped hold of Rob's arm, clutching more at the fabric of his shirt sleeve than him.

With an exaggerated action, Rob placed a finger on his lips. Jan's eyelids narrowed, her head shaking.

"Who's dog is that?" The animal pauseed and placed its attention directly on them. "In our garden. I'm not cleaning up the land mines, that's for sure."

Rob waved her down like a conductor trying to control a belligerent orchestra. Only the fox was alert, yet it didn't run. Instead, it lowered itself, belly settling on the grass, watching them both through ghostly eyes.

"Are you going to sit there and do nothing with that beast fouling our garden?"

"Wait, will you," Rob's whisper faded; he found himself lost in the predatory stare. Jan's chair scraped the flagstones as she hauled herself upright. Rob, too, pulled himself up, his heart thudding.

"Shoo, you beast, get out of here, shoo!" She took a few unsteady steps, arms outstretched with no apparent purpose. The fox leapt up, darting at Jan before changing direction and moving more to Rob and finally spinning itself in the direction it had emerged. There was enough time for Jan to give a disarticulated groan before she mis-stepped and fell to the spongy lawn. Rob gained ground, attempting to take hold of her as she collapsed, but it was too late, only grasping the tip of a shoe as her legs rode up over herself.

"Oh - you beast," she cried from her prone position on the grass, but the fox had gone, its tail slipping snake-like into the density of the hedge, leaving only the sound of cracking stems and branches as it made its escape.

"What are you doing, Jan? That was beautiful."

"Beautiful? How can you say that? It attacked me. You saw it. It went for me, almost trampled me to the ground."

"Come, Jan. Are you alright?" He pulled her up. She was a lot heavier than she used to be. A bright green smear from the mown grass stained the front of her dress.

"Look at this." Her hands flapped at the fabric in a vain attempt to wipe the streak away. "A beautiful pest, if you ask me. Who lets a big dog roam around people's gardens. I've got a good mind to call the police. I bet that idiot from number thirteen has something to do with this. He has more dogs than he can handle at the best of times. It wouldn't surprise me if he was some kind of puppy farmer. I'm going to report him if it's his. It nearly had me by the throat. Who knows what it's capable of? We aren't safe, Rob. On our own property as well!'

"Jan, it wasn't a dog."

"You're not telling me it's cat, are you, because I won't believe you. Not that size, not in this country."

"Jan," he tried again. "It was a black fox. They're very rare. We were lucky to see such a thing."

"What are you talking about, Rob? Foxes aren't black. It was some breed of dangerous dog. They breed them for fighting. I heard about it all on the radio only last week. Apparently, these illegal fights are happening all over; it's the evil under our noses."

Rob led her to the table, her weight on him from her inflated limp. He eased her into the seat, where she immediately picked up and began slurping her wine. Rob breathed deeply while she drained the liquid.

"Aren't they bad luck if they cross your path? That's what my mother told me?"

"That's a cat." He said as he sat reclined, taking his wine in hand. What was the point in pressing his case? It had gone. There had been so many visitors in their garden over the years, but a fox-like that was a rare treat. The odd deer poked its head through, and that was special enough. Why did she have to spoil those little things? "My father saw one once. I remember him telling us about it when we were kids. He was very ill, so we were never sure if he saw it or not."

"It's a bad omen. Running at me, out of the blue. Vermin! You'll have to use antiseptic on your lawn now; you won't believe the germs it's carrying. Ponder that while you think about how amazing it was. It's a bad sign. I just know it."

"I thought it was majestic."

"Majestic," she repeated in a mockery of his voice. "You see if an awful thing isn't about to happen. I'm never wrong. The news is going on about the environment. Then there is the nuclear talk with the Soviet leader. That was front-page today.

It says Nato has asked the US to remain calm. I can barely sleep anymore, Rob. Not with all the worries. I sometimes wonder what kind of world Jessica would be living in if…"

Rob looked, to the rusted table's folds and then up at the darkening clouds moving closer.

"Rains here. The garden needs it. I can't remember the last time it had a good watering."

Jan scraped at the green mark on her dress, before filling her glass almost to the brim, the dark liquid flat against the sides. She leaned in, sipping at the top before lifting it with care and studying the sky herself. He studied the thick crescents of dirt wedged under his nails from a morning of weeding. She gave a shiver. A tiny drop of red ran down the curve of the glass to rest on the stem before she brushed it with a finger, giving a tut as she did so.

"I'd like to know if it came from a neighbour's garden. I'll complain if we find a hole in their fence, allowing pests in. I won't stand for it." She tipped the wine into her throat while taking Rob's far away stare into consideration. "And don't you go encouraging it. I know what you're like." Jan finished her drink. "Let's go inside, before the weather comes in. That show starts soon." She was on her feet, bottle retrieved, the limp gone as she made her way to the door. The locks crunched as she battled, struggling to get a decent grip with her hands full as they were. Finally, it gave under her waggle. That was another job he had meant to get around to completing.

There was so much left to do.

"It's an evil sign if you ask me." Jan grumbled before climbing through the door.

He was right; the clouds were rolling in across the backyard, thick with a downpour. Jan finished pulling the door closed; her face peered through the glass to see if he was moving. Rob watched the first droplets of rain stain the fence posts. He waited against the sudden chill and the pinpricks of damp on his skin. As the heavens opened, exploding with unexpected ferocity, he sat. Still, observing, intent on any sign, knowing the black fox waited. The nape of his neck tingled. Maybe it was a sign.

"Rob," he screwed up his face at her noise. The television had clicked onto the chatter of nonsense which they so often filled their evening. "Rob!"

The residue of red spluttered the sides of his glass with uncountable raindrops, hair stuck to his face, but yet he didn't move from the spot. Maybe he shouldn't tell her. It wouldn't change anything.

*****

A haunting cry snatched him from sleep. At first, he thought it was their child. After all these years, when the worst of it had faded, a part of their young life held on tightly. After a moment in the darkness, taking in the age of it all, the cramp in his toes, his wheezing breath and Jan's snorting slumber, which was undoubtedly a deep and restful sleep despite her claims, he heard it again. A far-off cry, like a child complaining for its mother, animalistic, yet mimicry enough to slip into his dreams and remind him how things may have been different. If only their daughter had survived.

Hazily, he swung his reluctant feet to the side, desperate to shake the crackling snapshots of their little girl from his thoughts. Slippers noisy next to his dry skin, the bed rocking under him, ready to tip him over onto his book laden side table. After the second attempt, he shifted enough weight forward to get him standing, the cold freedom, a second skin. When he tugged at his nightgown, it snagged his aching fingers, joints clicking uncomfortably.

Through the hallway window, clouded moonlight highlighted the patterns from his lawnmower. The invisible rain trickled on the guttering. Darkness sat next to his trimmed borders and his freshly painted shed. Everything was still, and yet there in the absent light, something shifted.

Initially, there was only a large male. It padded, taking centre stage, head raised to sniff at the air before glancing behind. Then there were many, drifting out like puppets in a silhouette show, darting from dark recess to another before they took shape next to each other. A gathering of foxes meandering in an ever-changing circle. It had to be the entire family. How would it be possible to not have a closer look? A once in a lifetime opportunity, surely. He half considered waking Jan, but then reconsidered this possibility. What benefit would she derive from seeing these creatures? He wouldn't have enough disinfectant anyway.

He left the lights off downstairs and pulled the patio curtains to get an unobstructed view of the animals, keenly aware they would have vanished after his laborious navigation of the stairs. As if waiting, directly ahead, a large fox stood proudly. It didn't start or cower with surprise, as he may have expected. Instead, it lifted itself to meet his gaze. Rob froze against the drumming in his chest, careful not to scare the creature and frighten it off. Carefully, he bent down. His knees clicked with fury the closer he got to the carpet, grimacing as he lowered. Rob fancied he could reach out and touch the beads of water dripping off the large button nose and run his fingers through its coat. Each hair arranged so perfectly, jaws pressed together. Then its teeth appeared. Pointed canines, ragged and sharp, thrusting as the creature pulled back its gums.

"Come now," Rob whispered. "It's all fine. Everything is

fine. There is nothing to worry about. I'm here to watch, is all." His rising heart thrummed in his inner-ear. "Don't panic." His voice reverberated shakily off the glass.

Another fox, nothing more than a black shadow, appeared, or possibly it had been there all along. Its fire pit eyes leaned closer before being pushed aside by another set and then another until countless orbs of red floated ahead of him. Rob found himself on his rear. The creature's head loomed much higher than his own, his legs a dead weight by their presence. Fear clogged his arteries, pounding at his head, gripping his chest. The unfairness overcame him as his heart spluttered.

Frailty was a weakness. There was no threat here, no need to take the man by force, only to pry him from the disease inside. He turned, leaving the old man's body lying behind the invisible wall. For now, the chest moved, but there wouldn't be much time. The minor part that was Rob screamed out, making him stop, taste the air just in case. Then he ran through thickets, sliding along overgrown brambles, brothers and sisters spreading out, each signalling through the darkness. Still, the man fought him, confused, questioning before pleading to be free. He willed him to understand, but the patterns between them collided. Eventually, he decided there was nothing to do but ignore the gnawing curls of the man's life still stretching through him. Scratching at the earth gave little pleasure to the man. Neither did the thrill of the run through the open fields, but there was a fearful gift yet to give. This would wait until after he fed.

The sky was clear apart from the floating paleness above, and the cool night breeze had carried the rain away. Only the dampness of his fur reminded him. His family gathered looking for understanding in the things the Ancient One had shown them, but no more could they figure this than they understood the workings of the vast machines that ploughed fields or the concept of the enormous metal birds flying through the sky, and so they held their heads together and howled out, while the man cowered, niggling into his spine.

In the open, he pushed his muscles, leaping, diving until peace settled through both himself and the thing that was the man, more, a flicker of enjoyment enriched him, warm and nourishing until hunger groaned in his stomach. Leaning closer to the soil, he smelt the passings of a rabbit. It's droplets, fresh and acrid. With an arched back, torso lowered, he stalked through raised mounds of grass until he stood near the stream, keeping downwind. Water trickled as he waited, as still as the smooth pebbles and moss coated boulders. Then, the flattening of ferns to his side, the wide trunk of a buck, its nose lifting to the fresh air. Jaws snapped, clacking at the space the buck had stood. Darting one way then the other, each step out of reach before it disappeared into a clump of roots. He sniffed, snout compressed against the ground. There was nothing to be done while his stomach heaved at him with greater demand. Time to return, aware he would soon need to present himself. Down into the den, sweet decay brushing free from the bulging ribbons of root with their many stories, older than any of them as the man inside struggled at the closeness, uncomfortable with the confides, thrashing with a desire to be out in the open, but the Ancient One demanded a man, and it had chosen him to serve.

Deeper he goes, until he finds his mate, waiting with a mound of flesh under her sprawled body. Blood delicious against her. Ignoring all that was not him, the scream of another species trapped inside, he grabbed at the meat, biting, ripping, swallowing until his belly bulged. Not fresh as he preferred. He considered it as he lapped the blood from his muzzle, working his tongue between his teeth to free chunks of skin and gristle, tired, almost ready to lie, almost forgetting his purpose, the man whimpering like a pup. Then the call of the Ancient roared for attention.

It was not a voice or a scent, but a rumbling urgency that pulled him to his feet as generations before had served, so it was his time. His mate nuzzled him, uneasy. The tiny bones they left cracked under their tread. All his senses shook as The Ancient One demanded his presence, booming with a heavy impatience for the part of the man he carried. There was no choice but to take him.

Entrenched, swollen veins from the trees above wrapped around the network of tunnels. Deeper, he squeezed his frame through the narrow gaps, where earth had caved in from time to time, and they had dug at the aged pathways once more. He didn't enjoy this place. The man relished it less, crying for freedom as he reached the opening and its strange glow, but this was not done. Past the littered objects on the dirt, trinkets from above brought by his father and his father's father in a long line of prizes stretching beyond what he knew. Strange possessions, many of which refused to rot or crumble with age, lurid colours mottled with growth, scentless in the underground bunker.

Carefully, he stepped over the twisting pale vines, like the tips of maggots embedding themselves into the flesh of an old kill. With each step forward, they retreated, bodies swelling as the dirt closed around them, leaving mounds of upturned soil behind them.

Closer to the Ancient One. The ground rumbled, earth shook free from the walls until he crouched down, waiting for it to emerge. His ribs clattered the ground as he panted, a struggle to take in any air. If the man was still there, he was silent, waiting with the shared agony of anticipation.

Maybe he had held the man for too long. A curiosity edged his head forward, lifting it into the gloom. As enormous spines split the ground in all directions, the ends, huge weathered stones. The part of him who was the man forced him to look. It was no good closing his eyes, as a ditch can't control the water it contains, nor could he hide this new desire to see the unthinkable. Even as a menacing stir shuddered around him, he faced the jagged rocks, the edges rupturing, pale wires stretching out into the darkest corners and a sound like teeth snapping bones. He attempted to give himself over with all the will he had, but the man still fought until the Ancient One moved towards them.

Despite its shape, it wasn't of his pack. Limbs dangled from chords of flesh, white tubes entwined bone and protruded through the shadowed ribcage in a writhing mass, the thickest of which had squeezed into the base of the skull, its coil visible through the decayed eye socket. The Ancient One towered above them, suspended by more of the thick, colourless strands, like the stems of a thorn hidden from sunlight. It wasn't of his kin, but many beasts woven together. The mouth moved, a lopsided groan of rotted flesh and patches of fur, pungent with death, but when it spoke, its voice was everywhere.

An explosion of scent and colour burnt inwards, clawing with spider's legs at the insides of his mind. It dragged at the man, summoning him forward. He tried to resist, paws stepping back; this was not a fit end for any animal, but the Ancient One clutched at them tighter still. They both howled out as the Ancient One tested them with an endless weariness.

He saw his father, leading the family with the muscled shoulders he had envied. His father dropping wounded in the very spot they stood. The Ancient One, a hideous rotten flower dangling off its bleached stem, the core buried far underground, picked at the remnants. Then there were the fields before houses, and his first young gathered around in a ball of bodies, too many, some never to survive. Images beyond quantity, many outside of his memory. Ropes lowered a small box, resembling a tree smoothed, into the ground. The man's pain ached more than any flesh wound, a single loss filling him with emptiness; a single moment which changed everything.

A throbbing artery groaned. A new clarity formed with

explosions of light, as the charred sky buzzed with burning insects, so far into the forgotten, it was beyond the beginning, so unfamiliar. A colossal shape lumbered through barren stretches of burning rocks. It lay, not through tiredness, but of absence, of loneliness so deep it carved itself into the rubble, shifting its shape as it left the scorched landscape behind.

The man trembled with it all, causing him to shake his mane. He tried to leave, to take them away, but it grabbed, forcing the man to view, to answer for something, a time not now but soon which only the man fully comprehended—this the reason for their summoning.

Smooth shapes gliding skywards, birds plummeted, engulfed in flame. The Ancient lingered over details, contorting the pictures until it understood. This time the human inside reached out, demanding his answers as they both raged at the other with a ferocious intensity. The burden of it all crushing his skull, strength fading, and then it's stranglehold released.
The walls quaked, deep and resonating around them, similar to the cackling of a man. Tentatively, he turned, not sure it would allow their escape or if there was energy enough, but nothing restrained him. As he scrambled through tunnel after tunnel, he called to the man, but there was no response. If he heard, he sat deep inside, brooding over the last things it had shown him, reordering the confusion.

It would be easy to return to his mate, to lie next to his family safe and warm. Impossible, he knew the anger of the man, and feared him staying inside. The only thing he could do was return him and let the disease eat.

Back through the fields, to the line of houses, he travelled. Tired of it all and of the new visions which blurred his movement. Pictures of an endless bright and a never-ending dark. Of ragged hardship and everlasting stillness. All he had was a desire to return to the pack, enjoy their flesh next to his own. Home was all that mattered. There was time enough for this.

When he returned, the early morning sunlight reached across the garden, the first birds singing with saddened voices at the things to come. The man's chest still moved, although the rest of his bulk was still. He waited after the release, wanting to see movement. He owed him that.

Rob lay against the carpet. Two unblinking burning coals met his own eyes from the other side of the glass. He lifted his arm, desperate to make peace, but his muscles struggled. The fox turned, disappearing out of sight. Rob lay, reflecting on the horror to come, a dream of the end. Finally, he was still.

*****

Her hand pressed into his own. A warm and puffy, bloated sack squeezing at his claw. Jan leaned into his view. Muffled sounds dipped between clarity and obscurity. The swaying pasture of the fields, the beating wings of birds overhead, her racing heart pulsing with panic, were a cacophony.

"Rob," she called again. "Can you hear me?"

Numbness flattened his muscles, his sides ached from the hardness beneath him.

"Say, anything." Her voice cracked. "I'm calling an ambulance." He grabbed at her.

"Don't," he managed. "No time. Help me up."

"I can't move you. Rob, we need an ambulance. Don't you understand!"

She pulled his hand to her chest. He ached, with the slight movement he managed. Jan knelt. Salt water trickled. Only she was all the Jan's he had experienced from the beginning. An expression of youth, her skin as aged as them both, her words as insistent as they always had been.

"I thought you left me." She wiped the tears from her face. "What were you doing downstairs, looking for that bloody monster in our garden, no doubt. You should know better than to sneak around at your age. What will I do without you?"

"Hold me."
Despite her better judgement, she wrapped an arm under his head, shifting him forward, his joints popping with the pain. He understood where the darkness lurked, waiting for them all, not from some underground demon or a relic from a distant world, but from themselves. Their greed, and inability to exist without destruction, had brought about the end.

"I'm fine, Jan. I'm not going to the hospital. There's no point."

"Stop it. Stop this. It's scaring me, Rob."

"Don't be. It's all going to be fine." He did his best to smile, not the painted expression he'd worn for all those years, but one born of understanding, of perceiving where true wealth belonged; their journey carved through the richness of life.
A scream erupted from the street outside. A woman's desperate anger in the limited time they had left. Stumbling from the news as others sat around their television screens in silent panic.

Jan made to get up, pull back the curtains, and see the panic, but it would do them no good.

"Don't leave me, Jan."

"What's happening?" Her mouth wide, eyes complete circles of incomprehension.

He looked to the large patio windows, to the green of his tiny patch of land, to the fields beyond, and wondered how deep their warrens were.

"I never talked about our daughter. I'm sorry if I robbed you of the chance. Tell me. Talk to me of all the things you ever wanted to say. I want to imagine our family."

Her body shook, tears warm on her cheeks as she buried herself into his chest, their bodies together.

It was nothing but grumbling from the deep at first. The walls moaned, photos clattered, and then he knew. After this first wave of bombs, more would follow, retaliation until they returned the world to the charred mess of its conception, leaving a lonely giant to walk once more.

The heavens, a burning amber, growing lighter, highlighting the stillness ahead, an image of life created by an artist, frozen in a single moment, and then with a bright flare, it disappeared.

Printed in Great Britain
by Amazon